"Quick. We'll shelter
here from the storm."

As Gabe pulled Jonni close under an outcropping of rock, his lips met hers.

Thunder rocked the ground beneath her feet, but Jonni didn't know the difference between it and the tremors of desire that shuddered through her system. The lightening paled in comparison to the golden flame his devouring kiss ignited.

Her hand sought the silken smoothness of his slick wet hair. His hat got in the way of her curling fingers. Gabe reached up and flicked it away. Then his hand was back on her spine, arching her into the ever tightening circle of his arms.

"Gabe, please!" Jonni gasped. Trevor had been an expert in the art of love but he'd never turned her bones into putty the way Gabe was doing now....

JANET DAILEY AMERICANA

ALABAMA—Dangerous Masquerade
ALASKA—Northern Magic
ARIZONA—Sonora Sundown
ARKANSAS—Valley of the Vapours
CALIFORNIA—Fire and Ice
COLORADO—After the Storm
CONNECTICUT—Difficult Decision
DELAWARE—The Matchmakers
FLORIDA—Southern Nights
GEORGIA—Night of the Cotillion
HAWAII—Kona Winds
IDAHO—The Travelling Kind
ILLINOIS—A Lyon's Share
INDIANA—The Indy Man
IOWA—The Homeplace
KANSAS—The Mating Season
KENTUCKY—Bluegrass King
LOUISIANA—The Bride of the Delta Queen
MAINE—Summer Mahogany
MARYLAND—Bed of Grass
MASSACHUSETTS—That Boston Man
MICHIGAN—Enemy in Camp
MINNESOTA—Giant of Mesabi
MISSISSIPPI—A Tradition of Pride
MISSOURI—Show Me

MONTANA—Big Sky Country
NEBRASKA—Boss Man from Ogallala
NEVADA—Reilly's Woman
NEW HAMPSHIRE—Heart of Stone
NEW JERSEY—One of the Boys
NEW MEXICO—Land of Enchantment
NEW YORK—Beware of the Stranger
NORTH CAROLINA—That Carolina Summer
NORTH DAKOTA—Lord of the High Lonesome
OHIO—The Widow and the Wastrel
OKLAHOMA—Six White Horses
OREGON—To Tell the Truth
PENNSYLVANIA—The Thawing of Mara
RHODE ISLAND—Strange Bedfellow
SOUTH CAROLINA—Low Country Liar
SOUTH DAKOTA—Dakota Dreamin'
TENNESSEE—Sentimental Journey
TEXAS—Savage Land
UTAH—A Land Called Deseret
VERMONT—Green Mountain Man
VIRGINIA—Tide Water Lover
WASHINGTON—For Mike's Sake
WEST VIRGINIA—Wild and Wonderful
WISCONSIN—With a Little Luck
WYOMING—Darling Jenny

THE MATING
SEASON

Harlequin Books

TORONTO • NEW YORK • LONDON
AMSTERDAM • PARIS • SYDNEY • HAMBURG
STOCKHOLM • ATHENS • TOKYO • MILAN

The state flower depicted on the cover of this book is native
sunflower.

Janet Dailey Americana edition published January 1987
Second printing May 1988
Third printing June 1989
Fourth printing June 1990
Fifth printing August 1991
Sixth printing September 1991

ISBN 0-373-89866-5

Harlequin Presents edition published May 1980
Second printing February 1982

Original hardcover edition published in 1980
by Mills & Boon Limited

THE MATING SEASON

CHAPTER ONE

THE COUPLE WALKED unhurriedly along the curved corridor of the airport terminal. Tall and willowy, the woman was unconscious of the attention she was receiving from the men she passed. Her ash blond hair, a little longer than shoulder length, was cut in a windblown style that framed her face and its features of picture perfection.

Her jeans were of polished cotton in a bold, jade green color. A sweater jacket of black suede and knit was belted at the waist, permitting only a glimpse of her green and black print blouse, which was open at the throat. Her black boots were high heeled, clicking on the polished floor.

The man at her side matched her graceful, long-legged strides. He was only an inch or so taller than she was. His gray topcoat carried an expensive label inside, as did the charcoal suit beneath it. With dark, almost black hair, he was as good-looking as she was in a polished sort of way.

As they approached a newsstand in the terminal he caught her hand and drew her inside to the magazine rack. Standing out among all the magazines was the cover of a fashion magazine. It was a portrait, caught forever by the camera, of the woman now gazing at it. Glistening lips held the hint of a smile while blue eyes radiated the brilliance of inner pleasure.

He took a copy from the shelf to examine the cover more closely. "Another magazine cover for your already full scrapbook." He cast her a sideways glance that was both assessing and admiring. "Jonni Starr, the hottest model in the country. How does it feel to have the most sought-after face?"

Jonni smiled somewhat wryly. "It doesn't feel any different until someone asks me a question like that," she admitted. She stared at the photograph on the magazine cover, knowing the face belonged to her yet seeing a stranger. "Sometimes it feels as if the woman is someone else, not me."

"There's only one Jonni Starr." He crooked a finger under her chin to lift her head and bring her eyes level with his. There was a teasing glint in his look. "And I don't care what your birth certificate says, I still believe your agent made up that name."

Soft laughter rolled from her throat. It was the same accusation Trevor Martin had made when they first met almost two years ago. They had met at a theater party for a new Broadway show Trevor had produced, one of Jonni's rare evenings out.

"My mother will verify it for you, if you like." She repeated the same two-year-old answer. "Jonni was the closest she could come to naming me after my father, John Starr."

"I promise I'm going to ask your mother about it when I meet her," Trevor warned, but with a smile. "I'll buy this magazine for her. Since it's only just come out on the stands, she probably hasn't seen it yet."

"She'd like that." Jonni smiled her agreement with his thoughtful gesture. Trevor would have little difficulty charming his way into her mother's affection, but Jonni knew her father was a different matter. She waited while Trevor walked to the cash register and paid for the magazine. Trevor was a persistent and determined man. It had taken him two years, but he had finally won her over.

When she had first met him, Trevor had seemed too charming, too sophisticated, too worldly to be trustworthy. She hadn't been impressed by his wealth. The Starr family of Kansas, with its oil and cattle, could have matched him asset for asset. The expensive presents Trevor had showered her with did not turn her head.

When Jonni met Trevor she lived in the spacious and beautiful apartment she had occupied since arriving in New York six years ago. The rent was paid by her father until her modeling income allowed her to take care of it herself. She shared the apartment with a fellow fashion model, strictly for reasons of companionship, not for financial help. There had been nothing material Trevor could offer Jonni that she didn't have or couldn't get.

His status in the social and theatrical circles of Manhattan had not made an impression on her, either. At their first meeting Jonni was already a highly paid and highly recognized model. She didn't need the reflection of his power and success to give herself importance, so the usual ploys hadn't worked with her. She had kept Trevor at arm's length until he had eventually proved that his attentions were serious. It gave Jonni a secure feeling to know it had been a conscious decision and she hadn't been swept off her feet.

Tucking the magazine under his arm, Trevor returned to her side and curved an arm behind her waist. "Shall we go and claim our luggage and find that air charter company? Or would you rather relax and have a cup of coffee at the restaurant first?"

"No coffee for me, thank you." Jonni glanced at the large wall clock in the Kansas City terminal. "We still have to fly all the way across the state. I don't want to run any risks of arriving after dark—the runway at the ranch isn't equipped with lights for night landings."

"There's plenty of time," Trevor assured her, but he didn't argue any further as he directed her down the corridor toward the baggage claim area. At a row of telephone booths he stopped and suggested, not for the first time, "Are you positive you don't need to call your parents so they'll be expecting us?"

"No." Jonni negated that suggestion with a firm shake of her head. "I want to surprise them," she insisted.

A raised eyebrow showed that he disagreed with her. "Surely there are some preparations that will be necessary before our arrival. I don't think it's right for us to come without giving them some warning."

Jonni just laughed at that. "What you don't

understand, Trevor, is that in this part of the country the latchstring is always out. My mother doesn't need to get ready for company. She's always ready, just in case. Besides, I don't want the red carpet rolled out. I want to go home without any fanfare."

"It's one thing for you to do it. You're the daughter. But what about me?" he pointed out. "What kind of an impression am I going to make as their future son-in-law?"

"I don't want them to know I'm bringing my fiancé home." She didn't attempt to check her frank admission. "When mother and dad meet you for the first time, I want it to be without any preconceived ideas about what you'll be like."

"What you mean is that they won't be prejudiced toward the man who's stealing their daughter from them." Trevor flashed her a smooth smile as they continued along the corridor.

"More or less," Jonni agreed. "Once they meet you, I know they'll love you. Besides, they're both eager to have grandchildren."

"Not too eager, I hope," he murmured dryly. At her quizzical look, he explained, "I'd like you all to myself for a while."

"If I haven't forgotten some of the things I learned in my rural upbringing, such things take time." The gleam in her blue eyes laughed at the serious tone of her answer.

"So I've heard." Trevor's glance was both worldly and indulgent.

Her gaze dropped to the engagement ring on her finger. An enormous diamond solitaire reflected a rainbow of lights. "I only wish you hadn't been so extravagant over this ring. It's so huge it's almost obscene!"

Trevor did not appear concerned by her vague criticism. "I wanted it to be large enough for anyone to see it. There can't be any question that you belong to someone, namely me."

"No one could miss seeing it." Jonni adjusted the ring on her finger, not accustomed to the heavy weight.

"I've never claimed modesty as one of my virtues," Trevor admitted without remorse. His innate arrogance was part of his special brand of charm. Jonni accepted that, even though it irritated her at times. "I'm grateful you aren't cursed with any sense of false modesty. You're beautiful and successful, and you know it." An idle curiosity flickered across his handsome features. "I've never asked what your parents think about your career."

"They're proud, naturally." Jonni shrugged. "In their eyes, I could never do any wrong."

"Then why are you so concerned about them finding out about me before the fact, so to speak?" questioned Trevor.

"Because they'd ask where we'd live after we're married, and I'd have to tell them New York," she explained. "They still regard that as a terrible place to live, with muggings, rapes and burglaries going on all the time. I haven't been able to convince them any differently."

"Didn't you mention that they'd visited you in New York?" He looked amused by her comment.

"Yes, I usually see them twice, sometimes three

times a year. But this is the first time I've been back to Kansas since I left for New York six years ago." It didn't seem that long ago to Jonni. Yet, at the same time, it seemed much longer. Conflicting statements that were still true.

"Any particular reason?" he asked.

"The first year I was in New York, I didn't want to go back until I'd made some kind of success. When I did, I didn't have time to go back. If mom and dad hadn't visited me so often, I would probably have arranged to have enough free time to come home," Jonni admitted. "With Gabe in charge, it was easier for mom and dad to visit me."

"Gabe? Who's Gabe? I don't remember his name being mentioned before," Trevor commented with a thoughtful look.

"Gabe Stockman is dad's general manager." They arrived at the baggage claim area and Jonni's thoughts veered from Gabe Stockman. "There's the carousel with the luggage from our flight," she said, pointing.

When their luggage was retrieved from the rotating rack, Trevor signaled for a porter. The porter guided them to the gate where the chartered, twin-engine aircraft was waiting to fly them across Kansas to the Starr Ranch. They climbed aboard while the pilot stowed their luggage in the baggage compartment.

"All buckled in?" the pilot inquired, glancing over his shoulder at his passengers in the rear seat as he settled into the left seat.

"Yes," Jonni answered, but Trevor responded with only an uninterested nod.

"It'll just take me a couple of minutes to run

through this checklist and we'll be on our way,'' the pilot promised. He was past middle age, all crisp and professional with a decidedly military air.

The next few minutes were filled with revving motors and lifting ailerons and flaps. Then the pilot requested permission from ground control to taxi. A staccato response over the radio gave him taxiing instructions.

When it came their turn to roll down the runway, Jonni felt that familiar exhilaration. As the plane's wheels left the ground and tucked with a thump into the belly of the aircraft, she experienced a leap of excitement that came with flying. She glanced at Trevor, who was passively looking out the window as the plane gained altitude, then settled back in her seat, realizing Trevor didn't feel the same tug at his heart because she was the one winging her way home, not him.

Soon the plane turned west, crossing the Missouri River and flying over the flat wheat lands of eastern Kansas. After six years of living in the concrete city of New York, where the closest Jonni had come to grass and trees was Central Park and occasional forays into the surrounding suburbs, she suddenly realized how much she missed the wide-open feel of the country.

Below, the ground was laid out like a patchwork quilt in fields of varying shades of brown and green. The green of spring was tinting the pastures. The horizon stretched almost limitlessly without obstruction. The vastness of the sky was a clear blue, broken only by a puffy cloud and the glare of the sun.

The drone of the engines had made conversation difficult, but Trevor made an attempt. "Rather monotonous, isn't it?" he remarked, referring to the almost unchanging landscpae below them.

"Concrete buildings are monotonous. Mother Earth is always changing her clothes," Jonni corrected without trying to argue. His expression revealed disagreement and she laughed. "Not everything west of the Allegheny Mountains is wasteland, Trevor."

"No, there's Los Angeles," he conceded dryly.

"Look below," she instructed. "We're flying over the Flint Hills. Aren't they fascinating?"

"If you say so." But his agreement was strictly an indulgence, not an endorsement. "I'm still waiting to see a sunflower. Kansas is the Sunflower State, isn't it?"

"Yes, but they don't grow all year round," Jonni chided him,.then smiled. "I should be grateful you didn't get it mixed up with Iowa, the Corn State."

If Trevor had exhibited more interest Jonni would have pointed out the route of the old Santa Fe Trail, which had wound the breadth of Kansas in the pioneer days. Instead she kept silent, watching the changing terrain the plane's shadow covered. When the plane banked southwest, the lowlands of the Arkansas River were beneath them. Farther along the river, out of sight, was the historic town of Dodge City where the trail herds from Texas had driven their beef to the railhead.

They were nearing Starr country, where the Cimarron River snaked through the red hills. It was too soon to look for the ranch boundaries yet.

Jonni leaned back in her seat. So much of the flight had been in silence that she glanced at Trevor to see if he was still awake. He was, his gaze steadily watching her.

"I'm glad I insisted on taking two weeks off," she said. "It's going to be good to be home for a while. Are you certain you can't stay longer than the weekend?"

"I definitely have to be back by Tuesday," Trevor stated. "Business, my dear. Besides, I would rather arrange to spend my free time on a long honeymoon than share it with you chaperoned by your parents. From all you've told me, they sound old-fashioned."

"Yes, but they're very nice. You'll like them," Jonni responded with total confidence. Being old-fashioned was a trait Trevor made fun of, but it was also one he admired. Jonni was fully aware that part of her appeal had been the fact that she hadn't been easy to win. Once he had won her, he had no intention of letting her go, which suited Jonni just fine.

"Couldn't you stay a couple of extra days?" she asked. Saturday and Sunday would speed by so quickly. He would barely have time to become acquainted with her parents before he left. "I'd like to show you around the place."

"I'm afraid not," he replied without hesitation. "It would probably be all very interesting, but the great outdoors is not my style. A view from the air is sufficient."

Jonni knew that and had become resigned to it. "Daddy will want to show you the operation. He's quite proud of what the Starr family has built."

"I promise you I'll be dutifully attentive and interested when he does," Trevor assured her in a dryly mocking tone.

"You absolutely can't stay longer?" She repeated the statement as a question.

"I absolutely can't." Trevor took hold of her hand and carried it to his lips. "We haven't even arrived and you're already missing me before I leave. No wonder I'm in love with you!"

"I love you, too, Trevor," Jonni murmered.

Her hand curved itself to his strong jaw. His skin was tanned brown by the rays of a sunlamp he kept in his apartment. She knew he had a sunlamp because she had made use of it herself on one or two occasions. Leaning over, she placed a lingering kiss on his mouth.

The changing pitch of the engine's drone informed her that they were losing altitude, beginning their descent. She straightened back to her own seat, exchanging a warm look with Trevor as the pilot partially glanced over his shoulder.

"We'll be coming up on the airstrip soon," he told them.

After rechecking her seat belt to be certain it was securely fastened, Jonni glanced out the window. She was positive they were flying over Starr acreage even though it had been six years since last she saw it.

"Do you know what kind of condition this private runway is in?"

"It's a grass runway, but you can be sure it's in the best condition. My father has always insisted on that," Jonni replied with quiet authority. "It's on that plateau just beyond the buildings coming up on the right."

"I hope your parents are home," Trevor remarked. "I'd hate to think we've come all this way only to find out they're on vacation."

"Don't worry, I talk to them every week. Last Sunday they were very definite they wouldn't be going anywhere until the heat of the summer," she reassured him.

The white, two-story building of the main house stood like a quiet sentinel of the plateau. The branches of the towering trees that surrounded it looked bare from the plane's height, but a new carpet of green grass was on the ground. Hay was stacked in great mounds near the barns and equipment sheds. The red hides of Hereford cattle dotted the rugged land around the ranch yard.

The pilot cautiously made a pass at the landing strip to inspect its condition. A warmth of pride spread through Jonni as the statement she had made echoed true. The grass strip was in flawless condition, freshly mowed as if they were expected. The wind sock on the small metal hangar was barely moving. Painted on the roof of the hangar was a large star, to signify Starr Ranch. The next time around, the pilot set up for the actual landing.

"It's quite a walk from the airstrip to the main house," Trevor observed. "I hope you aren't planning a late-afternoon stroll."

"Someone will hear the plane land and come to investigate. We'll have a ride," Jonni stated prophetically.

With flaps down for a soft field landing, the

pilot slowed the aircraft to near stall speed and gently set it down on the grass runway. Short of the end of the strip, he turned the plane and taxied it to the hangar, cutting the engines. As the pilot climbed out to help his two passengers disembark, a pickup truck braked to a stop at the building and a tall man dressed in Levi's, Stetson and a denim jacket stepped out.

"You've landed on a private airstrip," he announced in a low-pitched voice that could border on a growl with the right intonation. At the moment it was only a politely worded demand to state their business or be gone. "There are several municipal fields in the area I can direct you to— unless you're having mechanical problems."

"I have chartered passengers for the Starr Ranch," the pilot replied evenly.

"Passengers?" The word was snapped out in wary disbelief.

At that moment Jonni stepped out of the plane onto the wing's steps. A throaty laugh came from her, rich with happiness to be home, yet controlled in its jubilation.

"Stop trying to order me off before I've even had a chance to set foot on home ground, Gabe," she declared in mock reproof.

She was met with silence as she negotiated her way off the wing. Standing on Starr grass, she lifted her gaze to the man standing near the wing tip. It was Gabe Stockman, who managed the ranch for her father.

Accustomed to being around men of her stature or only slightly taller, Jonni discovered she had to look up to meet his gaze, a fact she had forgotten in the passage of six years. Broad-shouldered, with a tautly muscled stomach and hips, Gabe Stockman was on the wrong side of thirty. The sun had weathered his hard-bitten features to the color of finely-grained leather, tanned and smooth, with wavy lines at the corners of his dark eyes from squinting into the Kansas sun. A neatly-trimmed mustache, as black as the hair beneath his dusty hat, grew above his upper lip, neatly trimmed and clipped.

The steady gaze of his eyes boring into hers, inspecting and appraising the changes of six years, was disconcerting to Jonni. There was something so frankly sensual about the way he was studying her that it made her nervous.

"Aren't you going to say something, Gabe?" she prompted to end the silence, which was beginning to make her uneasy.

His mouth quirked in that familiar, hard way, a corner disappearing into the edge of his black mustache. "It's about time you came back."

That warm feeling of coming home enveloped Jonni again. Gabe wasn't a stranger. He was a comfortable friend from the past, someone who had taunted her unmercifully about the boys she dated, who had mocked her ambition to become a famous model, but who had always listened to all her troubles, no matter how large or small.

"Is that any way to say welcome home after six years?" She laughed and crossed the space that separated them.

Her arms curved naturally around his neck as she rose on tiptoe to kiss him. Automatically his large hands reached to grasp her waist, their size spanning her rib cage. Her lips had hardly touched the smooth mouth beneath the black velvet strip of hair when his grip tightened fiercely on her ribs, nearly cracking a bone. She exhaled a faint gasp of pain, feeling her breath mingle with the warmth of his. Her heels rocked onto the ground as Gabe relaxed his grip, his face losing all its expression.

It was on the tip of her tongue to ask him what was wrong. Too late, she realized her mistake. She was no longer in New York where people who were practically strangers hugged and kissed in greeting. Gabe's inbred aloofness would not permit so demonstrative a greeting. She smiled and tried to ignore the incident.

That was easy, because Trevor was walking toward her. Taking a step away from Gabe, Jonni turned to include him, stretching out a hand to be enclosed in Trevor's grip.

"Gabe, I want you to meet Trevor Martin, my fiancé," she introduced him, and saw Gabe's dark eyes narrow in piercing inspection. "Trevor, this is Gable Stockman, the manager of Starr Ranch."

"I'm pleased to meet you, Mr. Stockman. Jonni has mentioned you often," Trevor lied smoothly. He hadn't learned of Gabe's existence until that day.

He offered to shake hands but Gabe was already turning to look at Jonni. She couldn't tell if Gabe was deliberately ignoring the outstretched hand of her fiancé or didn't see it. But she had never been able to read his expression. His was the perfect poker face, masked and unblinking in its regard.

"I suppose he's the reason you finally came home," Gabe observed with a grimness that implied censure.

Anger flashed in Jonni that Gabe could be so rude as to talk about Trevor as if he wasn't standing right there. "Trevor is the main reason I've come home now," she admitted. "He only proposed to me last week." She moved closer to Trevor's side. "Naturally I wanted mom and dad to meet him right away."

"I tried to persuade Jonni that we should call ahead to let them know we were coming," Trevor explained, "but she insisted on surprising them. I hope Mr. and Mrs. Starr are here. They haven't gone away for the weekend, have they?"

"No, they're at the house." It was a clipped, precise answer, without elaboration or comment.

"Aren't you going to offer us your congratulations?" Jonni challenged, irritated and off balance because of his attitude.

"Congratulations," Gabe responded in a flat voice, devoid of emotion. His gaze flicked to the huge diamond in her engagement ring. "Don't wear that around the animals, it's liable to spook them." He issued the warning with a straight face, minus any humor, even the derisive kind.

Gabe brushed past Jonni and Trevor to take charge of the situation. "We'll load them in the back of the pickup." He picked up one of the heavier cases and started to reach for the seond, of an equal size, when he glanced back to see Trevor still standing beside Jonni, making no move to help. Gabe altered his choice to one of the lighter bags. With a nod of his head toward the remaining heavy bag, he said, "You can bring that one, Mr. Martin."

Jonni felt Trevor stiffen in resentment. A second later, he changed his mind and walked over to take the second suitcase. Her lips thinned into a straight line as her gaze met Gabe's shuttered look.

She was caught in the middle, aware of both sides of the situation. Trevor had been accustomed all his life to having someone else do the heavy work. It was a natural oversight on his part to let Gabe and the pilot carry the bags.

On the other hand, Gabe was not a hired hand. He was the ranch manager, in total authority. He carried no man's luggage and would not assume the role of servant for anyone, not even a guest. He was Trevor's equal, willing to help but not to do it all.

What bothered Jonni was the terse way Gabe had put across his point. It could have been accomplished with a bit more finesse, less bluntness. If Gabe had used friendlier wording Trevor would not have bristled. Jonni suspected Trevor might have even apologized for his oversight. Now there was an open breach between the two men. Jonni blamed Gabe, knowing he could have been more tolerant.

With the luggage arranged in the back of the pickup the pilot climbed back into the plane. Its twin engines were revving up as Jonni slid into the cab of the truck. She sat in the middle between the two men, her shoulders rubbing against theirs. Trevor held her hand in his, affectionately winding their fingers together. When Gabe reached forward to start the engine, his gaze flicked to their entwined hands. Jonni noticed the way his square jaw hardened in disapproval.

"Where are you from, Mr. Martin? New York?" Gabe shot out the question, making the foregone conclusion become a condemnation. There was a harsh, abrasive thrust to his voice that reminded Jonni of the serrated edge of a knife blade.

"Manhattan, yes," Trevor replied, and added deliberately, "Manhattan is in New York City."

Gabe shifted the truck into gear and parried the gibe, coldly smiling. "I've heard that. What do you do for a living?"

"I have several interests—investments in real estate, office and apartment buildings and the like, as well as some stocks and a few Broadway productions."

"It sounds as if you won't have too much trouble taking on the added responsibilities of a wife." The remark sounded offhand and indifferent as Gabe slowed the truck to make the curve in the dirt road ahead.

"I doubt that I'll have any trouble," Trevor said with blatant arrogance. "It will be a case where two can live as cheaply as one, since we won't have two apartment payments along with food and utilities."

"Do you mean you aren't living together already?" Gabe issued the question with the lazy surprise of someone expecting to hear differently.

"No, we are not!" Jonni's cheeks flamed as his gaze slid slowly over the two of them. Jonni blamed the heat on outraged anger and Gabe's total lack of tact, rather than embarrassment, which was usually alien to her.

She shifted in her seat, trying to inch closer to Trevor before the curve in the road slid her toward Gabe. Pain stabbed in the area of her rib cage. By morning, her flesh would probably be marked with bruises where Gabe's hands had gripped her for the punishing instant.

"I don't think you know Jonni very well, Mr. Stockman," Trevor stated, coming to her defense.

"I don't think *you* know Jon very well." Gabe abbreviated her name, the glint in his dark eyes indicating an inner secret not to be shared with Trevor. " 'Johnny be good' used to be the catchword for Jonni around here. It was more often a plea."

What Gabe said was true, but not the way he implied it. She had always been too curious, eager to explore new territory, riding farther afield on the ranch than she was usually allowed. She was bold, not wild.

The bend in the road was negotiated without Jonni sliding into Gabe. Ahead of them was the house, her childhood home. The skeletal branches of the trees were dotted with green buds. Spring was only a few warm days from bursting out in a tide of green. Gabe stopped the truck at the end of a stone path leading to the house.

"How long are you planning to stay?" He addressed the question to Trevor as he swung his long frame out of the cab.

"I'll have to leave on Monday. Jonni is staying for two weeks." This time Trevor didn't need to be prompted, and walked to the rear of the truck to remove two of the suitcases.

Without the pilot to assist them, Jonni offered to help. "I'll carry some."

Gabe handed her the two lightest ones. "Two weeks isn't a very long time, compared with six years." There was condemnation in his brooding look. "What does that break down to? Two and a half days for every year you've been gone?"

"I was lucky to arrange that," she defended.

"That face is very much much in demand." Trevor smiled at her with pride.

Lifting the last of the bags over the tailgate of the truck, Gabe appeared unimpressed by the statement. "I don't think the world would come to an end if she took a couple of months off."

"It could seriously affect her career, though," Trevor murmured with faint arrogance.

"So what?" Gabe said with an offhand shrug. "She'll be marrying you. Or are you going to continue working after you're married?" The question was directed at Jonni.

"Well, yes, naturally." She glanced at Trevor, who smiled encouragingly. "Why shouldn't I?"

"I wouldn't dream of suggesting that Jonni give up her very successful career simply because she's marrying me," Trevor inserted.

Gabe's gaze raked Trevor from the top of his head to the polished tips of his shoes, as if doubting his manhood. There was something dismissive about the way Gabe turned away from him, a disgusted sound coming from his throat.

Rage flared in Trevor's expression. He took a

step toward Gabe as if to challenge him. "Don't." Jonni whispered the warning. She knew who would be the victor in a fight, and it wouldn't be Trevor. He had neither the muscle nor the experience. And for all his determination, Jonni questioned that he could be as ruthless as Gabe was.

With remarkable restraint, Trevor schooled his expression to blandness. He cast Jonni a stiff smile and indicated with a nod of his head that she should precede the two of them to the house. As she walked along the stone path she visualized the two men walking behind her. She was struck by the startling contrast between the two.

Both were tall and dark, but Gabe was rough with all blunt edges; Trevor was smooth and polished, like a fine gemstone. Trevor was dressed in an expensive, hand-tailored suit and topcoat and fine leather shoes; Gabe wore ever durable denims and boots worn down at the heel. Trevor was sophisticated and well mannered, fully aware of which fork to use at the most elaborate table setting.

Gabe said what he thought, leaving no one in doubt of his opinion. Shrewd and uncannily intelligent, he had obtained most of his education from life while Trevor had attended the best schools available, including two years at a European university. Both were unmistakably men, one refined and the other the raw product. Jonni felt slightly shaken by the comparison and didn't know why.

Before Jonni reached the steps to the porch the

front door opened and her father walked out, tall and slim, his blond hair silvering to gray. A look of incredulous delight beamed from his handsome face.

"I saw you coming up the walk and couldn't believe my eyes!" he declared.

"Surprise!" she laughed.

He paused to shout into the house. "Caroline! It's Jonni! She's come home!"

CHAPTER TWO

THE NEXT FEW MINUTES were lost in a confusion of laughter and hugs. Everyone was trying to talk at once with no one understanding what anyone else was saying. If her father hadn't noticed Trevor standing quietly beside Gabe, the chaos might have continued longer.

"Who's the young man you brought with you?" he asked, drawing her mother's gaze to Trevor, as well.

Before Jonni had a chance to make the introduction, Gabe identified Trevor. "This is her fiancé."

Jonni hurried to fill the sudden silence that followed his announcement. "Mom, dad, this is Trevor Martin, my fiancé," she acknowledged Gabe's statement. "Trevor, this is my mother, Caroline, and my dad, John Starr."

Trevor shook hands with each of them, exhibiting his charm as he lingered over her mother's hand. "Now I understand where Jonni inherited her looks. It was obviously from you, Mrs. Starr. May I call you Caroline? Mrs. Starr seems too formal. Mother Caroline might be appropriate, but you don't look old enough to be my mother—or my mother-in-law, for that matter."

"Flattery will get you anywhere with me, Trevor." Her mother laughed at the lavish compliment. "And please, feel free to call me Caroline."

"Thank you, Caroline." Trevor made a mocking half bow over her hand.

Jonni accidently glanced at Gabe during the exchange between her mother and Trevor. She saw the look of disgust that flashed across his expression, quickly concealed by a shuttered mask falling into place. *Damn him*, she thought angrily.

"I can't get over it, John. Our little girl is engaged." Caroline shook her head in disbelief, smiling and catching her lower lip between her teeth as if expecting it to quiver.

"Now don't go crying over this, Caroline," John Starr ordered, putting an arm around his wife's shoulders and giving them an affectionate shake.

"I'm not. I'm happy," was the reply. A questing pair of blue eyes turned their attention to Jonni, their shade the same vivid blue as her own. "You do love him, don't you? What kind of a question is that?" Caroline Starr remonstrated with herself for asking it. "Of course you do, otherwise you wouldn't be marrying him."

"I do love him, mom." Jonni said the words anyway, knowing they would reassure her mother. She raised her left hand to offer her engagement ring for her parents' inspection. "See?"

"It's beautiful!" her mother breathed.

"It's as big as a spotlight," her father remarked, and glanced at Trevor. "She'll have you in the poorhouse if you let her keep picking out jewelry like this."

"Jonni is worth it." Trevor smiled at her, but didn't bother to explain that the ring had been his choice, not hers.

"Good heavens, what are we doing still standing on the porch!" Caroline exclaimed. "Come inside. John, bring your daughter's suitcases in."

As they entered the house Trevor said, "I hope our arriving so unexpectedly won't cause you too much inconvenience."

"John and Caroline won't tell you if it does," Gabe inserted in a cool, dry voice.

"Don't listen to him," Caroline spoke up, dismissing Gabe's remark with a wave of her hand. "We never know when we're going to have company, so we're always ready. My daughter—and my future son-in-law—would never be an inconvenience to us anyway. Let me hang up your coat for you, Trevor."

As Trevor shrugged out of his topcoat Jonni saw her father eyeing the suit and tie Trevor wore. In this part of Kansas, men dressed much more casually. Ties, especially, were reserved for more august occasions. John Starr had never been one for formality.

"Which suitcases are yours, Jonni?" Gabe interrupted her thoughts. "I'll carry them up to your room."

"All but the two tan ones with the brown straps." That left four containing her clothes.

Gabe's raised eyebrow was the only indication that he questioned why a man who only intended to stay for three days would need two suitcases, but the question wasn't voiced. Jonni found it impossible to explain to Gabe how meticulous Trevor was about his wardrobe. Everything had to coordinate perfectly. Then she became irritated that Gabe was making her feel an explanation was necessary to justify the amount of luggage Trevor had brought. She pivoted away toward her mother, trying to conceal the anger in her expression.

"Will I be sleeping in my old room, mother?" she asked.

"Yes, dear," was the smiling answer. "I thought Trevor could take the guest room at the end of the hallway. Will that be all right?"

"Fine," Jonni agreed.

"Let's go into the living room." Caroline Starr began to move in that direction. "I'll fix some coffee. Or would you rather have something to drink?"

"I think what they would like," her father intervened, "is some time to rest and freshen up after that long plane trip here."

"Of course. How foolish of me!" Caroline stopped, her teeth biting at her lower lip in chagrin as she glanced apologetically at Trevor. "You must think we're terrible hosts. I don't have any excuse, except that it's so wonderful to have Jonni home again that I don't want to let her out of my sight."

"I can fully understand that, Caroline." Trevor smiled, inclining his head in agreement. "I feel that way about her myself."

The adoration in his response was calculated to draw a pleased smile from her mother, and it succeeded. "I'll take you upstairs and show you your room," Caroline offered.

"There's no need, mother. I know the way. Why don't you put some coffee on instead?" Jonni suggested. "Trevor may want a drink later, but I'd love a cup of coffee."

"I'll fix some," her mother agreed.

As Jonni turned toward the stairs, she saw Gabe had separated her luggage from Trevor's. Her weekend bag was tucked under an arm. He was already holding one of the heavier cases and he was reaching for the other. Her cosmetic case still sat on the floor.

"I'll take this one, Gabe." Jonni bent to pick it up.

"I planned on that." His expressionless reply reinforced his statement that he took it for granted she would carry part of her own luggage.

The absence of any protest, even a polite one, thinned the line of Jonni's mouth. Gabe seemed to be implying that if she thought she was going to be waited on like a celebrity, she was wrong. Jonni expected nothing of the kind and resented him for thinking she did.

The sparkle of veiled temper was in the glance she swept to Trevor. "This way," she said to him. She added over her shoulder to her parents, "We'll be down shortly."

Gabe was four steps up the stairs before they started. Jonni sent daggers into the broad expanse of his tapering back. Under the weight of the suitcases his muscles bulged to fill the shirt. Yet he carried the cases with seemingly little effort. At the top of the stairs Gabe paused to wait for them, his sun-leathered face impassive in its expression.

"Your room is at the end of this hall, Mr. Martin." The rolled brim of Gabe's Stetson dipped toward the right.

"Thank you." There was a faintly condescending ring to Trevor's voice.

"There's an adjoining bath, shared with the other guest room, which is unoccupied at present," Gabe stated. Caroline always keeps fresh towels in it."

"I'm sure it will all be satisfactory." But the glittering light in Trevor's eyes indicated he thought Gabe knew too much about the house and its routine. It was a stiff smile he gave Jonni. "I'll meet you downstairs in twenty minutes or so."

"All right," she agreed.

As Trevor started down the hall to his room, Jonni turned in the opposite direction toward hers, but Gabe and the width of the suitcases he carried blocked her way. She saw the dark, calculating look that watched Trevor walking away, and immediately a wary feeling stole through her.

"By the way, Mr. Martin—" Gabe's low, drawling voice halted Trevor's steps "—Jonni has probably forgotten after six years, but the floorboards there in front of John's and Caroline's door squeak rather loudly. You might want to keep that in mind if you're planning any late-night wanderings." The implication, of course, was "to Jonni's room."

A nerve twitched below Trevor's left eye, betraying his incensed reaction to the information. There was an instant of electric silence before a smiled curved his mouth.

"Thank you, I'll remember that," he said. With

the next step he took the floorboards creaked loudly under his weight. Trevor hesitated for a split second before continuing on his way.

Gabe turned toward Jonni's room but she saw the deadly smile of satisfaction on his face before he completed the pivot. She did a slow burn as she followed him to her bedroom and closed the door. Anger simmered to the forefront when Gabe set her luggage down and turned to face her. The blue sparks shooting in her look didn't seem to interest him greatly.

"If I were a man, I'd punch you in the mouth, Gabe!" Jonni declared, issuing the statement through tightly clenched teeth.

Amusement flickered briefly in his eyes. "Your fiancé doesn't appear to share your opinion. Maybe that says something about him."

"Trevor is a gentleman. He doesn't feel it's necessary to resort to violence over a mere insult," she retorted.

"I suppose he thinks it's beneath him." Gabe's mouth curled into the black mustache above his lip. Almost instantly, his gaze made a leisurely appraisal of her figure, lingering on the agitated rise and fall of her jutting breasts. "Of course, if you were a man, Jonni, this situation would never have occurred." His gaze lowered to take in the rounded curve of her hips. "Even without the Gucci label on your jeans, I can tell you aren't a man."

A tremor shivered through her nerve ends at his blatantly sexual look. "They aren't Gucci jeans." She denied the designer label for want of a more cutting response.

Contemptuous amusement was in his quick ex-

halation of breath. "They sure as hell aren't
Levis." His long strides carried him past her to
open the door leading into the hallway.

"Damn you!" Jonni choked on a mixture of
hurt and anger. "I almost wish I hadn't come
home!"

Gabe paused in the doorway, impaling her with
a hard, cynical look. "We can agree on that. I'm
beginning to wish you hadn't come back, too." He
walked out of her bedroom, punctuating his sentence with the closing of the door.

Jonni wanted to throw something at the door to
vent the aching rage inside her. But it was a
childish impulse and she wouldn't submit to it. She
turned her back on the door, digging her long
fingernails into the palm of her hand until the
subsequent pain made her relax the fist.

In a burst of agitated energy, she set the cosmetic case on the dresser and began unpacking the
contents. Below, she heard the banging of the
screen door shutting. The window beside the
dresser faced the front of the house. Dotted Swiss
curtains of pale yellow were drawn from the window panes by ties in matching material.

Compelled by an invisible force, she stepped to
the window as Gabe emerged from the shadow of
the porch overhang. His unhurried, rolling gait
gave an impression of lightness that was unusual
for a man his size. It reminded Jonni of the unob-
trusive stealth of an animal.

A tightness gripped her throat. Her homecoming hadn't lived up to her expectations and it was
Gabe's fault. His discordant welcome had set the

tone, throwing everything else off-key. Why? What had gone wrong?

What had happened to that invisible link that had always made her feel close to him? Had it ever existed in anything other than her imagination? Maybe in the past six years she had created in her mind the idea that there was some special bond between them. What had her relationship to Gabe been? Not friends—the gap in their ages precluded that. Not brother and sister, either, since Gabe had never permitted her to be that familiar with him. Jonni found that she couldn't define their relationship because she didn't know what it had been.

Once, in her teens, she remembered that she had attempted to idolize him. But as soon as Gabe realized it, he had figuratively removed himself from her pedestal and crushed the puppy adoration in its beginnings. He had destroyed the dream she had tried to build around him with a callous indifference that had bordered on cruelty. After that painful experience, Jonni had never again made the mistake of fantasizing about him as a lover.

What did that leave? Jonni couldn't find a label that fit. In her confusion she watched the tall, well-muscled figure walking toward the pickup truck. Black hair, black eyes, black mustache, all that was familiar to her, even the features that had hardened to shut out the world. Yet Jonni had the feeling Gabe was a stranger, that she didn't really know him at all, and never had.

At the sound of her bedroom door being opened Jonni stepped guiltily away from the window as if she had been caught doing something she shouldn't. Her behavior irritated nerves that were already raw. She had nothing to hide, especially not from Trevor. As he entered her room his gaze narrowed curiously, having caught her furtive movement away from the window.

"Hello, darling. Is your room all right?" She attempted to assume a bright facade to mask her previous reaction to his entrance.

"It's comfortable, yes." He walked to the window where she had been standing and looked out.

Glancing sideways, Jonni saw Gabe walking around the pickup to the driver's side. He opened the cab door and paused to look up at the window. The wide brim of his Stetson no longer shadowed his sun-bronzed face. His features were drawn in a grimly set expression before his chin came down and the hat brim shielded his face once again.

"He's an insolent devil," Trevor remarked.

Looking away from the window, Jonni didn't pretend that she didn't know whom Trevor was referring to. The metal slam of the truck door closing echoed into the room. She began arranging the bottles of lotion, perfumes and powder in the proper order on the dresser top. "I wouldn't say that to Gabe's face if I were you," Jonni murmered.

Trevor laughed shortly and without humor. "I have no intention of doing so," he assured her. "Not that I wouldn't like to back it up with a pair of brass knuckles, just for the sheer pleasure of ramming my fist down his throat!".

"If I'd given it a thought, I would have warned you Gabe doesn't know the meaning of the word 'tact,' " she offered ruefully.

"I would have been better prepared." He moved to stand behind her, lifting aside her pale amber hair to nibble at the curve of her neck. "I expected an inquisition like that about my background and our future plans from your father—not a hired hand."

"Gabe is a hired hand only in the loosest meaning of the term, like an executive in one of your firms," Jonni corrected, and shrugged a shoulder in vague protest against the exploring caress of his mouth.

Trevor straightened to take her by the shoulders and turn her to face him. "I didn't realize it was a touchy subject with you, too." He studied her closely. Jonni squirmed inwardly at his piercing examination, although she didn't know why, since she had nothing to hide.

"It isn't that." She ran her fingers along the lapel of his jacket, unnecessarily smoothing the material. "I just don't want you to let something slip that might cause more ill feelings."

"You know me better than that," he admonished.

"I'm just being cautious. I want you to make a good impression on everyone." To make up for the way she had avoided his previous caress, Jonni let her lips seek his to initiate a kiss that his practiced skill would finish.

With studied passion he took possession of her mouth and drew her more fully inside the circle of his arms. Her lips parted under his. His hand slipped inside her sweater jacket to cup the rounded peak of her breast. Jonni yielded to the consummate experience of his embrace.

When his arm tightened around her to mold her more firmly to his male shape, it touched the bruised flesh near her rib cage, the injury Gabe's hands had inflicted. She broke away from the kiss, gasping and wincing at the brief but sharp pain.

"What's the matter, darling? Did I hurt you?" Trevor was instantly concerned and curious.

"My ribs hurt from the ride," she lied, loath to mention the incident with Gabe since it would accomplish nothing.

An understanding smile curved his mouth. "I don't know which was worse," he acknowledged, "the springs on that truck or the chuckholes in that so-called road."

"Probably a combination," Jonni suggested, and stepped out of his encircling arms. "The truck could never be mistaken for your Mercedes, although the condition of the road could rival what's found in New York."

"The driver wasn't your local drugstore cowboy, either." Trevor brought the subject back to Gabe. "Where does he live? Here in the house?"

"No." With the cosmetic case unpacked, Jonni set it on the floor and lifted the suitcase containing her lingerie onto the bed. "Dad took one of the bunkhouses and turned it into private living quarters for Gabe. Why?"

"He seemed to have such an intimate knowledge of the house." Trevor shrugged, then elaborated, "the location of your bedroom and the squeaking floorboards in relationship to the guest room."

"Gabe is practically a member of the family," Jonni replied a shade defensively. "He's free to come and go as he pleases. Besides, nothing escapes his attention, no matter how trivial," she explained. "He has an uncanny memory. He can be in a room once and remember every detail—the location of furniture, a sticking window, which drawer an item is kept in—everything."

"What was his reason for being in your room?"

Jonni didn't like the way Trevor was looking at her—or what he might be implying. "One of my windows was stuck and dad needed his help to get it loose," she snapped. "What did you think he might have been doing in here?"

"Hey, temper!" he chided with amusement.

"I resent your insinuations!" Jonni flashed, unpacking her lingerie and shoving the expensive lace garments in the empty drawers of her dresser.

"Why are you so upset because I briefly thought there might have been something going on between you two six years ago?" Trevor studied her controlled fury with alert curiosity. "Is he married?"

"No, he isn't married." Telling herself she was overreacting, Jonni tried to calm down.

"Then why get so upset?" Trevor wanted to know, but he kept the tone of his question deliberately offhand. "He has a kind of he-man toughness that might appeal to some women, especially adolescents. He looks as if he just stepped out of an advertisement for Marlboro cigarettes. Is it inconceivable that you might have developed a crush on all that brawn?"

"Brawn *and* brains. Don't make the mistake of underestimating his intelligence," Jonni warned. "It isn't inconceivable that I could have been infatuated with Gabe, but it so happens that I wasn't.'' She finally answered his question.

"I was just finding out where the competition is," Trevor said. "The last thing I want to do is compete with an old love from the past. I dislike being jealous of ghosts."

His explanation relaxed her. She abandoned her defensive attitude and smiled. "Gabe doesn't rank among my list of old flames, so you have nothing to worry about."

"Good. I'll feel more at ease about leaving you here alone for two weeks." He lifted a sheer nightie from her suitcase. It was brown, trimmed with beige lace. "Very pretty. Remind me to have you model this for me sometime."

His glance was deliberately suggestive, but it wasn't his unsubtle message that was sending a pleasant glow of warmth through Jonni. It was the prospect that Trevor could be jealous.

"You really thought it was possible that I might have loved Gabe, didn't you?" she marveled. "And it worried you."

"It concerned me." Trevor avoided the stronger word. "Is it so unlikely that you would have?"

"Gabe is so much older than I am, for one thing," Jonni pointed out.

"So much older?" He appeared skeptical of that reason. "He can't be more than thirty-seven, thirty-eight. And you're twenty-five. Twelve years, even thirteen years, is not that vast an age span. We're nine years apart. So, if you're trying to imply that Stockman is old enough to be your father, it would be unlikely even for a very precocious child."

"I...I suppose not," she conceded after a second's hesitation. "I guess Gabe probably seemed older because I was younger."

"Probably," Trevor agreed, and handed her the chocolate brown nightgown of thin silk he had admired. "Are you going to finish unpacking or shall we rejoin your parents downstairs?"

"I can finish unpacking later. Mom and dad are probably anxious for us to come down." Despite her reply, Jonni began to fold the nightgown neatly to lay it in the drawer.

When she did so, Trevor walked over to let his hands slide over her hips, careful to avoid her sore rib cage. His mouth made a slow trail across her cheek to her mouth.

"My lovely country sophisticate," he murmured, "with her silks and satins and fashion-designed jeans." He teased her lips with a nibbling kiss. "I should have thanked Stockman for warning me about those squeaking floorboards. It could have been awkward if your father had caught me stealing into your room in the middle of the night for a preview look at you in that nightgown."

"Trevor!" Jonni drew her head back from his kiss, a frown of protest creasing her forehead.

"Don't worry, love," he mocked her. "I won't embarrass you, although I admit to being tempted."

"Don't tease about things like that." She moved out of his arms, not seeing any humor in his remark. "I want my parents to like you. It's bad enough that you're from New York City."

"I suppose I would fare better if I were some

Kansas hick." Hidden in his voice was the sting of truth.

"I'm a Kansas hick," Jonni reminded him, resenting the term with a surge of pride.

Trevor didn't want to argue. Catching her chin between his thumb and forefinger, he planted a hard, silencing kiss on her mouth.

"You've become a beautiful, elegantly refined hick," he declared. "And soon to be Mrs. Trevor Martin—with your parents' approval and consent, of course. Shall we see what we can do about obtaining that?"

Pushing aside her sensitivity to the vaguely derogatory term, Jonni linked her arm with his and started toward the opened door to the hallway. Her return to her childhood home had started out wrong, but she was determined the day wouldn't end the same way.

CHAPTER THREE

"What will you have to drink, Trevor?" John Starr acted the host, handing Jonni her requested cup of coffee. "Besides coffee, we have some cold beer in the refrigerator and some whiskey in the cupboard."

"Whiskey, please, with a splash of water." Trevor hitched up his trouser legs as he sat down beside Jonni on the living-room sofa.

"A man after my own heart," her father declared in approval of Trevor's choice. "I'll have the same. My only allotted and prescribed alcoholic drink of the day," he added.

"Prescribed?" Jonni questioned his use of the word.

But her father ignored it. "If we'd known we had an engagement to celebrate tonight, we'd have bought some champagne and had it chilled and waiting to drink to the two of you." He walked across the braided rug that covered nearly the entire oak floor of the living room. "It'll take me a minute to get some ice and water from the kitchen."

"What did he mean, prescribed?" She addressed the question to her mother.

"It's that heart condition of his. Dr. Murphy

prescribed a shot of whiskey a day. It's supposed to help his blood or something. Can you believe it?" Caroline Starr laughed in a show of unconcern. "Those two men! One lies and the other swears to it."

"Is it serious?" Trevor questioned.

"When you get to be our age, nothing is ever dismissed lightly. But no, as long as John doesn't overdo it, he'll live to be a hundred," she assured them. "Luckily, Gabe doesn't give John a chance to do anything too strenuous."

"When was this discovered? Neither of you said anything to me." Jonni frowned.

"Not in detail, no," her mother admitted. "We glossed over it a few years ago when we told you John was retiring to take things easier. He doesn't like to talk about it. It isn't easy for him, Jonni, to admit he isn't the man he once was. You have to understand that. Besides, it honestly isn't anything to worry about or I would have told you." Approaching footsteps forewarned them of John's imminent return, and Caroline Starr swiftly changed the subject. "Did you notice the new drapes, Jonni? I finally found some material that would match that unusual shade of blue in the sofa. The room is so much cooler in the summer."

"Yes, I saw them." Jonni followed her lead, glancing at the light blue drapes hanging at the windows. "And you've added to your collection of wood carvings." She glanced at the mantel of the fireplace. "That eagle and his nest are breathtaking."

"Wait until you see the old cigar-store Indian

John found in a junk shop. It's a treasure, isn't it, John?" She glanced at her husband with pride.

"To us, it is." He grinned back as he added whiskey to two glasses.

"It was in pretty bad shape," her mother explained, "but John managed to restore a lot of it. He has it in his den. We'll have to show it to you later."

"You've done a lot of changing since I was home." Jonni glanced around the room. The arrangement of the furniture looked the same, but there were two new chairs and a polished oak table that she didn't remember. The walls were a lighter shade of blue gray to contrast with the woodwork. "It all looks familiar, but with little differences."

The ensuing conversation became a discussion of the house and its contents, what had existed, been added or removed since Jonni had lived there. Each item seemed to make its own conversation, whether it was the leather recliner her father hadn't wanted to part with or the rickety antique table her mother had bought for a song and spent a fortune to restore.

When her father finished recounting his story about a massive Lincoln desk of walnut he'd bought only to discover there wasn't a door or window large enough to get it inside the house, they were all laughing.

Caroline Starr wiped the tears of laughter from her blue eyes. "As you can tell, Trevor, John and I share a passion for old things, not all of them necessarily deserving the word antiques. But we seem to get sentimentally attached to them all the same. I hope we aren't boring you with our non-sense," she said.

"Not at all," he assured her, and Jonni reached over to slide her hand over his, silently thanking him for not being bored by her parents' less than sophisticated outlook.

"We may not be boring him," her father inserted, "but I'll bet we're starving him. When will dinner be ready?"

Her mother glanced at her watch in surprise. "I didn't realize it was so late." She hastened to her feet.

"I'll help you, mother." Jonni started to rise.

"No, you stay here with Trevor," she insisted. "Everything is either in the oven or steaming. The table is already set. I can manage this time."

"I'm sure you can, but four hands—" Jonni began.

"Sit," her father ordered, his eyes twinkling. "Obey your mother."

"Yes, daddy." She smiled and sank back into the cushions beside Trevor, knowing it was a lost cause to argue with the two of them.

"You already have Trevor's ring on your finger. It's a little late now to be trying to impress him with your cooking. You still can cook, can't you?" John asked. "I remember some of your first meals. Fortunately you improved very quickly before we all acquired terminal ptomaine."

"Yes, I can still cook. And let's not bring up past disasters," Jonni insisted with a laugh.

"Has she fixed dinner for you yet, Trevor?" her father quizzed.

"Yes, a couple of times," he admitted. "But we eat out a great deal."

"I much prefer Caroline's cooking to anything served in a restaurant," her father stated. "Wait until you taste what she can do with a piece of beef. It absolutely melts in your mouth. Caroline is an excellent cook. Jonni takes after her."

"I enjoy cooking, although I haven't had the time or opportunity to do much of it." Jonni hoped it wasn't a skill she'd lost from lack of use.

"You will," her father winked.

Trevor noticed the vague apprehension in her expression and misinterpreted its cause. He squeezed her hand in reassurance. "Don't worry, honey, I won't chain you in the kitchen after we're married. With the uncertain hours I keep we'll probably still eat out a lot. It will be much easier than you trying to keep a meal warm until I get there."

"You don't exactly have banker's hours," Jonni admitted, and checked the sigh that trembled on her breath.

"John." Her mother appeared in the living-room archway. "You're going to have to come out to the kitchen and talk to Gabe. He feels he's intruding by joining us for dinner this evening. He insists he'll fix something at his place, but you know he can't even crack an egg."

"I'll speak to him." John's mouth thinned into a no-nonsense line as he left the room.

Caroline hovered in the doorway. "Gabe is so impossible sometimes," she said with a slight grimace of disgust. "He's been like a son to

John—you know that, Jonni. Why on earth would he get the idea that you wouldn't want him to have dinner with us?'' She continued to gaze in the direction her husband had taken.

It was the last thing Jonni wanted, but it was also the last thing she wanted to admit to her mother. She kept silent, knowing her mother didn't really expect her question to be answered. She darted a sideways glance at Trevor. His look held the same reaction she felt. He lifted her hand to kiss the back of it, a gesture of understanding.

At that moment her mother turned, seeing the exchange but not its meaning. ''Maybe if you spoke to him, Jonni, Gabe would get this ridiculous idea out of his head,'' she suggested.

''Oh, mother, really, I—'' The words of refusal came instantly, but Trevor interrupted them.

''Perhaps it would be a good idea, honey,'' he said. ''We wouldn't want Gabe to feel left out.''

Her startled look questioned his sanity but obviously he no longer regarded Gabe as a threat. Which, of course, he wasn't. Was he? The fact that she had asked herself that question sent a shiver of alarm down Jonni's spine. She did her best to ignore it.

''I'll see if I can persuade him to stay,'' she agreed, rising.

With a falsely cheerful smile at her mother, Jonni walked past her toward the kitchen. Before she reached it, she heard the placating tone of her father's voice although she couldn't make out the words. As she opened the kitchen door a fist slammed down on the counter top, rattling the dishes in the cupboard above with its force.

"Damn it, John! You don't know how the hell I feel!" Gabe didn't attempt to control the violence in his voice. Its emotional fury almost took Jonni's breath away.

"If you break mother's china, I can tell you how she'll feel," she declared with a shaky laugh.

Gabe's head snapped in her direction. An invisible shutter closed his expression, concealing the black rage she had glimpsed for only an instant. Her father wore a worried look when Jonni glanced his way.

"Have you talked Gabe into having dinner with us tonight?" she asked.

"Is that what you're doing out here?" Gabe responded in a low, taunting challenge. "To lend your persuasions to John's?"

His dark, expressionless eyes were leveled at her. Jonni wanted to look away, but she couldn't break free of an odd compulsion to return his gaze. There was a shaky fluttering of her pulse.

"Yes," she admitted. She assumed a bright pose as if staring into the dark lens of a camera instead of his eyes. "You know they want you to eat with us," she reasoned.

"What about you and your...fiancé?" He hesitated over the term, as if there was an epithet he would have preferred to use.

Bristling, Jonni curved her lips into a honey-sweet smile. "We want you to join us, too," she lied.

He smiled with one side of his mouth. The resulting expression conveyed amusement and derision. "Who am I to deny what Jonni Starr wants?" Gabe mocked.

"Then you'll stay?" The lilt of her voice made it a question.

A resigned sigh came from him as he turned away. "I need a few minutes to get cleaned up." Both his hands were on the kitchen counter. They seemed to be supporting almost his full weight. He looked and sounded very tired.

In a flash of sympathy at his apparent weariness, Jonni offered, "Can I get you a cold beer from the refrigerator, Gabe?" She saw the wicked, laughing look he gave her father.

"Maybe that's the answer, John. Maybe I should get rip-roaring drunk," Gabe suggested with cynical humor. To Jonni, he said, "No, I don't want a beer." Shoving himself away from the counter, he walked toward the rear of the kitchen. "I'll use the back washroom to clean up. Tell Caroline I'll be at the table whenever she's ready to serve dinner."

He puzzled Jonni. Everything about Gabe puzzled her. She stared after the man she had thought she'd known until the closing of the washroom door shut him out of her sight. Her confused gaze wandered to her father.

"What's the matter with Gabe, dad?" she asked. "What's wrong?"

He didn't immediately answer as he took a deep, considering breath and walked toward her. Draping an arm around her shoulders, he hugged her to his side for an instant, a sad smile curving his mouth.

"Gabe had a bad day, one of the frustrating kind where things happen that a mere human is powerless to prevent. It's been a long, cold winter, and a dry spring, so far. It gets a man down, even the strongest."

"I suppose that explains why he was so rude and irritable today." Jonni's mouth tightened, remembering how infuriating he had been. "But that's no excuse for bad manners."

"Under the circumstances, I hope you'll be a little understanding and overlook Gabe's bad temper." That same smile was still on his mouth. "After all, you're happy. You've got what you want—a tall, dark, handsome man and a ring on your finger." Keeping his arm around her shoulder, he walked her toward the door. "And that man is waiting in the living room for you. You'd better get in there and rescue him from your mother before she starts telling him all those stories about you when you were a baby!"

As always, he succeeded in coaxing a smile from her. "I love you, dad." She planted a kiss on his cheek before moving ahead so they could walk single file through the door. Jonni paused on the other side. "What do you think of Trevor, dad? Do you like him?" An anxious thread wound through her question.

"He seems to be a personable and prosperous man. But what's more important is your happiness. That's all your mother and I want—for you to be happy. Are you?" he asked, studying her.

"Yes, I'm happy. I'm very happy," she hurried to assure him.

"That's all that matters," her father insisted.

They entered the living room together. Jonni's

blue eyes were sparkling with pleasure at her father's ready acceptance of her choice of the man whe wanted to marry. Trevor lived in such a different world from the one John Starr knew that Jonni had thought he might be reluctant to endorse Trevor until he had an opportunity to know him better. Her attention was on the man smiling so warmly back at her and Jonni missed the concerned look of her mother.

"Did you speak to Gabe? Is he staying for dinner?" Caroline immediately began an interrogation.

"Yes, he's staying," her father answered. "Jonni and I talked him into it."

"What was his problem?"

As her mother asked that question aloud, Trevor rose to stand beside Jonni and whisper in her ear, "Did you use that famous Starr smile to change his mind?"

"And a personal invitation from you and me," she whispered back.

"Gabe's had a hard day." John Starr responded to his wife's question. "He didn't want his bad mood putting a damper on Jonni's celebration." He shrugged away the reason as unimportant.

"Where is he now?" Her mother looked toward the kitchen.

"In the washroom cleaning up." Jonni supplied that information. "He said he'd be only a few minutes and for you to serve dinner whenever you're ready."

"I'd better get the food on the table, then." She hurried to the kitchen.

Trevor glanced at his reflection in the mirror hanging on the wall opposite him. An ornately carved wooden frame surrounded the oval glass. It was an heirloom brought by the first of the Starr family to settle in Kansas, and was thus entitled to prominent display in the living room.

"Maybe I should have changed into a clean shirt," Trevor commented as he smoothed the length of his tie inside his jacket and inspected the result.

"No, you shouldn't have," Jonni responded.

His comment had drawn an amused and slightly derisive look from her father. She had explained to Trevor that her parents didn't stand on ceremony, but the habit to change for dinner was too deeply ingrained in him. He was simply too fastidious about his appearance.

"We seldom have reason to wear a suit and tie around here—" her father injected the comment their exchange "—except to church on Sunday."

"New York's dress code isn't quite that relaxed." Trevor turned from the mirror, a look of vague dissatisfaction about him.

It wasn't all that strict in New York. Jonni could have told him about a number of excellent restaurants and nightclubs that didn't require formal attire, and circles of people she knew who dressed casually. But what was the point when he didn't go to those places or associate with those people? She kept silent.

A few minutes later her mother asked them to come to the dining-room table. With an odd number at the table, a balanced seating arrangement was impossible. Her parents were at opposite ends of the rectangular table with Jonni and Trevor seated on one side facing Gabe. The arrangement was uncomfortable, but the alternatives weren't any better.

"How long have you two known each other?" Caroline Starr passed the sour cream and potato casserole while her husband carved the meat. "I know Jonni has mentioned you in her letters, Trevor, and when we've spoken to her on the phone, but...." Her voice trailed off so he could answer her first question.

"We met two years ago."

"That long?" Her mother looked surprised.

"It was hardly a whirlwind courtship." Jonni laughed and accidentally looked into a pair of hard black eyes across the table from her. There was a nervous fluttering in the pit of her stomach, ending her laughter, but she kept the smile on her face.

"She was most elusive," Trevor told her mother before smiling at Jonni.

"And he was most persistent." There was a teasing inflection in her voice, but little twinkle in her eyes.

"I regret that I never had the opportunity to meet you or John during your visits to New York to see Jonni. Unfortunately, I was always tied up with other commitments."

"If we'd suspected that it was serious between the two of you, we wouldn't have been so shocked when you arrived today," her father stated, laying down the carving knife and fork.

"How long will you be able to stay?" her mother asked, and instantly added, "I do hope you don't have to leave right away."

"I'll have to leave on Monday," Trevor began the answer.

But Gabe finished it. "Jonni is staying for two weeks." It was his only contribution to the conversation thus far. There something faintly condemning in his tone, as if he implied that Jonni expected them to feel honored she was staying that long. But she was the only one who seemed to notice his biting dryness.

"Two weeks. How wonderful!" her mother exclaimed. "We'll have time to make plans about the wedding. Have you set the date yet?"

"Not yet," Jonni admitted.

"Soon," Trevor stated. "After the length of our courtship, I don't think we need a long engagement."

"You would make a beautiful June bride," her mother declared, passing the platter of beef to Gabe. "That's only two months away. We'll barely have time to have the invitations printed. We'll need to speak to Reverend Payton, too, about reserving the church." As Caroline Starr began listing the arrangements that had to be made, it occurred to her that she hadn't consulted her daughter about a few major decisions. "You are planning a church wedding, aren't you?"

"Yes." The answer was hesitant as Jonni darted a sideways glance at Trevor and did her best to ignore the sharp, questioning look from the man seated opposite her.

Her mother looked from her daughter to her future son-in-law. "You were planning to be married here in Kansas, weren't you?"

"Actually we had discussed having the wedding in New York," Jonni admitted.

"But all our friends and family are here," her mother protested.

"Now, Caroline," her father interposed to calm his wife, "it's *their* wedding. And you must remember that they have many friends in New York, plus Trevor's family."

"I suppose so," she conceded. "I just always imagined Jonni walking down the aisle of the church where she'd been baptised and confirmed. There are so many endless details in planning a wedding—flowers, the wedding cake, gown fittings, the reception, wedding music. How will you ever be able to arrange all that, Jonni, and work, too?" Her mother made it sound an impossible task.

"We can have much of it done for us," Trevor stated. "There are professional firms that arrange entire weddings down to the last details."

Her mother's forthright nature ran unchecked. "But that's so impersonal!" Jonni tended to agree with her, but under the circumstances it was the most logical route to take. Across the table, Gabe was subjecting her to a narrowed look. "Part of the fun of having a big church wedding is picking out the little things like the cocktail napkins or the champagne glasses, or racing to the printers because a name is misspelled. It builds up the excitement to a wedding. The ceremony itself is usually an anticlimax."

"After all these years, I finally know how she felt when we exchanged our vows," her father joked.

"Oh, John, you know that's not what I mean," Caroline returned impatiently.

"What she means is—if you two are getting married in New York, the bride's parents will probably be moving there so she can take charge of the wedding." He continued to tease her even as he made the serious suggestion.

"That's a wonderful idea, mother," Jonni agreed with it. She laughed. "And it will certainly save on the expense of a lot of long-distance phone calls to Kansas."

"We could do that, couldn't we, John?" Her mother latched on to the suggestion with growing enthusiasm. "Gabe can look after things here," she added to enforce it.

Jonni slid a questioning look to Gabe, but his gaze was downcast, focused on his plate. A muscle flexed along his jawline, contracting sharply.

"That's right, Caroline. I'll see to the ranch," he agreed.

"It's all settled, then," the older woman announced with a lightened expression. "When you go back to New York, Jonni, will you look for a small apartment your father and I can rent for a couple of months?"

"There's no need to rent an apartment. Vickie, my room-mate, is moving out at the end of the month—the firm she's working for is transferring its headquarters to California. You and dad can have her bedroom." It was all working out so perfectly it seemed predestined, Jonni thought.

"That's ideal," her mother enthused. "While you're here these next two weeks, we'll have to start making up a list of family and friends we'll want to invite to the wedding."

"It's a bit early for that, isn't it?" her father asked.

"It's better than leaving it until the last minute," was Caroline's argument. "Have you looked for a place to live after you're married?" She addressed the question to both of them, but Jonni answered.

"There's no need to look. Trevor's apartment is centrally located and beautifully decorated. It's much roomier than mine, too. Wait until you see it."

"Have you been in it?" A faintly shocked expression registered in Caroline Starr's face at the thought that her daughter had been in a man's apartment.

"Yes, mother," Jonni replied, and refused to elaborate.

"Excuse me." Gabe rose abruptly from the table, his water goblet in his hand. "I need some more water."

"I'll get it for you," Caroline volunteered.

"I can manage," he insisted, halfway to the kitchen door.

His sudden departure left a confused silence, the rhythm of their conversation broken. It was several seconds before anyone attempted to resume it. Then it was Caroline.

"Wouldn't you rather have a house than an apartment, Jonni?" she asked. "A place with a lawn and some trees, your own space?"

"Naturally I would. But you don't find what you're describing in the middle of Manhattan," Jonni explained patiently. "An apartment is much more practical and convenient. You'll understand what I mean once you see Trevor's."

"Don't they have houses in New York?" her mother persisted.

"Of course they do. But they're mostly located in the suburbs, which means Trevor and I would have to commute. It's definitely more logical to live in the center of everything," Jonni insisted.

"But in the center of New York?" Her mother grimaced.

"I've been living there for the past six years," Jonni reminded her. "You make it sound like the cesspool of the world! New York is a vibrant, exciting city."

"It's so crowded and congested, a jungle of concrete. I should think you would miss the country. You were such an outdoors person," her mother declared.

"I still am," Jonni assured her. "I have my own horse and I go riding several times a week. I'm outdoors whenever it's possible. I go swimming at the beach, on weekends, and jog through Central Park."

"That's dangerous." Her mother frowned at her in sharp reproof.

"Not if you're sensible, mother." She tried not to smile in the face of her mother's genuine concern.

But the twinkling sparkle of amusement was in her blue eyes when she looked up at Gabe's return to the dining room. His black gaze looked and held hers. A funny breathlessness attacked her lungs, her heart flipping unevenly. It was really quite strange. The contact was broken as he pulled out his chair and sat down, placing the filled water goblet by his plate. Ice cubes tinkled delicately against the crystal sides.

"Actually, Caroline," Trevor was saying, "I'm more concerned about Jonni being injured while riding her horse than I am about her jogging through Central Park with her friends. I've tried repeatedly to persuade her to sell the beast, but she refuses."

"Where do you ride?" her father asked.

"Surely not in all that traffic?" her mother protested.

"They have riding paths," Jonni explained patiently. "So you see, I'm really still your little country girl at heart."

"You would never know it when she's in New York," Trevor stated. "She's smooth and polished, a real sophisticate."

"I don't think there's enough water in New York to wash away the dirt between Jonni's toes." Gabe ran an assessing eye over her that seemed a little too penetrating. Jonni wasn't sure that she wanted him to see that deeply into her. "It's part of her," he concluded.

"You could be right." Trevor's grudging admission indicated that he didn't like the idea of agreeing with Gabe about anything but for the peace of the table conversation, he would.

There was a lull in the conversation before her mother sighed, "I still can't get over the fact that our little girl is finally going to be married. I was beginning to think you would never find anyone and settle down, Jonni. Now, it's happened so suddenly that I don't seem to be able to believe it."

"Hardly suddenly," Jonni protested with a throaty laugh. "I've known Trevor for two years."

"I know you've mentioned him in your letters, but you never hinted it was serious between you." Her mother picked up the bowl of potatoes and offered it to Gabe. "More potatoes?"

"No, thank you." He took the bowl and passed it on to her father at the head of the table.

"I may work slowly, but I'm very thorough," Trevor responded to her mother's comment. "When I proposed to Jonni, I wanted to be certain she'd have no doubts about accepting."

"Just think, John." Caroline Starr beamed a smile to the man at the opposite end of the table. "We're finally going to have our grandchildren after all this time!" Her loving glance encompassed Jonni and Trevor. "I do hope you two aren't going to be one of these modern couples who wait years to have your children?"

Jonni hesitated, darting a look at Trevor. Planning a family was one of the few things they hadn't discussed. She had no idea what his views were on the subject.

Trevor laughed easily. "I think it would be better if Jonni and I were married before we become concerned about how soon we'll start a family." He had avoided a direct response and Jonni knew no more than anyone else about how he really felt about the subject.

"I think you'd better switch topics, Caroline," John Starr suggested, "before you end up asking something that might prove embarrassing to everyone."

"If you say so," she conceded, but couldn't resist adding, "I've never kept it a secret from Jonni how much I want grandchildren."

"Would you excuse me?" Gabe rose from his chair. "I have some paperwork to do."

"But what about dessert?" Caroline looked at him in surprise.

"Not tonight, thanks." His sweeping gaze included everyone at the table. "Good night." Grimness was etched into his features. There was a glimpse of anger in his eyes when they touched on Jonni. It ruffled her fur. She hadn't said or done anything to make him angry.

After the front door had closed, her mother said, "Gabe is pushing himself too hard, John."

"Nonsense. He's simply very conscientious." He leaned back in his chair and rubbed his full stomach. "Did you say something about dessert?"

CHAPTER FOUR

AFTER DINNER, Jonni and Trevor went for an evening walk. Hand in hand they strolled along the rutted lane. The air was brisk and the velvet sky overhead was littered with stars. Jonni's gaze searched out the Big Dipper.

"You'd better watch where you're going," Trevor suggested dryly, reproaching her star-gazing activities. "This ground is pretty rough and uneven."

"If I stumble you'll catch me, won't you?" she asked with a flirtatious tilt of her head.

"I intend to spend the rest of my life catching you," he told her with loving warmth.

Something black swooped down at them. Trevor flung up an arm to protect his face and ducked, but the object had already flown off into the night.

"What was that? A bat?" Anger ran in his demand.

Jonni laughed. "It was probably a bird."

He stopped and pulled her into his arms. "So you think I'm funny, do you?" he said in a mockingly threatening manner.

"I think you're a big, good-looking dude," she declared.

"A city dude who's very much in love with you."

His mouth covered hers in a long and satisfying kiss. She snuggled closer to the warmth of his body, sliding her arms inside his topcoat. It was very enjoyable in his embrace and it led her to think of other things.

"How do you feel about having children, Trevor?" she asked.

He shifted her to his side, keeping an arm around her as he started walking again. She fell into step beside him. It was too dark for her to see his face clearly, so she couldn't read his expression.

"Any plans for a family will definitely have to wait a while," he said. "We have to consider the effect it would have on your career."

"Why should it affect it?" She frowned at his answer.

"I don't recall seeing any pictures of pregnant women on the covers of *Vogue* or *Harper's Bazaar*," Trevor mocked.

"They're mostly face shots, portraits," Jonni argued.

"It wouldn't be wise to have to limit the kind of assignments you can accept. Besides, you're just reaching the peak of your success. It would be foolish to throw it all away. Your popularity won't begin to wane for another four to six years. We can think about a family then," he reasoned. The arm around her waist tightened in a reassuring hug.

"But by then I'll be in my thirties." There was

more risk involved in bearing children during those years.

"That's true," he acknowledged.

Jonni strained to see his face. A tiny shaft of fear splintered through her veins. He was staring straight ahead, not looking at her. A question loomed in her mind.

"Trevor, do you want to have children?" Jonni forced her voice to be calm.

He hesitated. "Naturally, I would like to have a son." But his voice lacked enthusiasm for the idea. He had said it because it was expected of him. Something died inside her and Jonni felt cold. "Brr!" Trevor shivered as if feeling the sudden drop in temperature, too. "It's getting cold out here. Let's go back to the house."

"Yes, I'm getting tired anyway," she agreed in a listless voice.

DRESSED IN A faded pair of denim jeans and a blue pullover sweater that showed equal signs of wear, Jonni tiptoed down the steps. Trevor was a late sleeper and she didn't want to wake him. It was early, only a few minutes past six, but she was accustomed to rising with the sun. Outside the birds were singing and the morning sun was warming the air.

At the bottom of the stairs she began humming to herself, a happy whimsical tune. She sauntered toward the kitchen. At this hour, that was where she would find her parents. The tips of her fingers were hooked inside the back pockets of her blue jeans. A silk scarf of blue and gold paisley print formed a wide band around her head. The ends escaped from the ash-blond length of her hair to trail over the front of her shoulder.

Her parents were seated at the small breakfast table when she entered the kitchen. They looked up, surprise changing to smiles at the sight of her.

"Good morning, mom, dad."

"Good morning, Jonni." The greeting was echoed in unison.

"You're up early this morning," her mother commented.

"I always am," Jonni replied, and walked to the refrigerator.

"We just finished breakfast. You remember how your father always likes to eat the very first thing after he wakes up. Can I fix you something?" her mother offered.

"No, thank you. I'll just have some juice." She took the pitcher of orange juice from the refrigerator and moved to the cupboard where the glasses were kept. As she filled one of the glasses with juice, she realized how comforting it was to find things still in the same places, routines unchanging. It rolled back the time to the years when she had lived here.

"Something more than juice, surely. How about some toast?" her mother suggested.

Jonni laughed. She had never been able to eat in the mornings, but her mother had always tried to persuade her to have something. Not even that had changed.

"This is all I want." She took a sip from her glass and winked at her father. "I have to watch my figure."

"I thought that was Trevor's province now," he teased dryly.

"Not yet."

"Is Trevor awake? Will he be coming down?" Her mother rose to refill the two coffee cups on the table.

"He's still in bed, I think," Jonni answered, and joked, "he's a city boy, accustomed to sleeping until a saner hour in the morning."

"I was up around midnight," her father said. "I saw a light shining from under his door."

"He was probably reading." Jonni shrugged the observation aside as nothing to be concerned about. She wandered to the window above the kitchen sink and drank the last of her juice. "It's a beautiful morning, isn't it?"

"It looks as if it's going to be a warm spring day," her father agreed.

"I think I'll go walk around. Explore a bit," Jonni said and set her glass on the sink counter. As she walked to the back door, she glanced over her shoulder and waved. "See you later."

Outside, Jonni followed the path worn through the lawn. Its route was the most direct line to the barns. The air was crisp, the sky a pale morning blue. The temperature was low enough that she was glad she'd worn her old pullover sweater over her long-sleeved white blouse. It kept the chill from her skin.

Shoving her hands in the front pockets of her jeans to keep them warm, she strolled toward the barns. She could smell the hay, its biting aroma mixed with the freshness of clean air. The large sliding door at the first barn was open.

From inside she could hear the noises of horses eating, blowing the grain dust from their noses and bumping the sides of their feed troughs to get every last grain. The warm, pungent scent of horses wafted through the door. It sounded crazy, but she liked that smell. It was like perfume to her, but she doubted that everyone would agree. Trevor didn't. She had always been careful to shower and shampoo when she returned from riding before seeing him.

Metal pails clanged together inside the shadowed interior of the barn. The sound came from the feed bin. Jonni paused inside the wide opening to let her eyes adjust to the absence of direct sunlight. The door to the grain room closed and she turned.

A man walked toward her, dressed in the rough clothes of a cowboy, his short legs slightly bowed. He hesitated in midstride when he saw her, then continued forward.

Gloved fingers reached up to touch his hat brim. "Mornin', miss."

As he walked past her outside, he carefully averted his eyes. Jonni smiled. She had forgotten how shy some Western men could be. There had been recognition in his first brief glance. He knew who she was, but he hadn't forced an introduction of himself, a gesture of respect for her privacy. Jonni had missed that in the six years she had been living in the east. There, it seemed only aggressiveness was recognized.

A bale of hay was dropped from above to land on the barn floor in front of her. It bounced once, sending up a cloud of chaff and dust. Some of it filtered into Jonni's lungs. She coughed and waved to clear the air she was breathing.

Looking up, she saw Gabe standing at the edge of the opening to the hayloft. His stance was relaxed, one knee slightly bent. His arms were at his side, leather gloves protecting his hands. Instead of a jacket, he was wearing a suede vest lined with sheepskin. Wisps of hay and chaff were clinging to the rough denim fabric covering his muscled legs. He looked tough and fit, a man of the West with his hat pulled low and that dark mustache shadowing his mouth.

Irritation simmered through Jonni as she realized he had tossed that bale of hay down without checking to see if anyone was below. But she hadn't been anywhere close so it was pointless to say anything.

"Good morning." Her greeting was sharp with a ring of challenge.

"You're up early this morning." He lifted his hat and settled it back onto his head in almost the same position as before.

"Why does everyone seem so surprised by it?" Jonni questioned with a surge of impatience. "First mom and dad, now you. I've always been an early riser."

"Were you? You've been gone six years. We've probably forgotten." His gibe at her prolonged absence struck a sore nerve, but he was already turning away before she could retaliate. "I've got a couple more bales coming down. You'd better step out of the way."

"You could have warned me the last time," Jonni retorted, and moved to stand close to the door.

"I saw you."

Jonni could hear his flat voice and the sound of his footsteps walking in the loft above her, but she couldn't see him. "You could have said something just the same."

"Like what?" Gabe appeared briefly in the loft opening to toss down the bale he carried, then disappeared.

"Like 'good morning.' It's considered good manners to greet people when you see them," she flashed after him.

Gabe came back with the third bale and it tumbled to the floor with the others. "Good morning." He recited the phrase she had prompted. He jumped down from the loft, landing on his feet like a cat.

Jonni shook her head in exasperation, frustrated and at a loss as to how to cope with his terseness. "Do you want to give me a hand with these bales?" Without waiting for an answer, Gabe picked up the nearest one and started toward the row of partitioned mangers.

Hesitating for a mutinous instant, Jonni walked to a second and reached down to pick it up by the parallel bands of twine. The taut string bit into her fingers as she tried to lift. It was too heavy. She could barely get it off the ground.

"It weighs a ton!" Jonni dropped it within an inch of where it had been, groaning from the exertion.

Gabe stopped, carrying his with little obvious

effort. "About eighty pounds is all. You're out of condition."

"Eighty pounds is all." She repeated his words sarcastically.

"Maybe less." He shrugged. Down the row of stalls, a horse stretched its neck over the manger and whickered at the delay. "Here." Gabe set the bale he was carrying on the floor. Deliberately he broke the twine to free the square bale of hay. "Put some hay in the mangers for the horses. I'll bring the other bales."

Jonni took a portion of the unbound hay and deposited it in the first manger. A chestnut horse plunged its nose into the strands. "Who was that man who left when I came in? Is he somebody new you've hired?" she asked as she walked back to the bale for another armload of hay.

Gabe carried the second bale farther down the line. "Ted Higgins. He's not exactly new—he's been working here four years now. He and his wife have rented the old Digby house. He was in town all day yesterday. His wife is in the hospital."

"Oh? Is it serious?" As Jonni emptied the hay into the manger and turned back for more, she fell in step beside Gabe.

He looked down at her, his expression cold and remote. "What do you care? You're only going to be here two weeks."

She stopped short, his response acting like a slap in the face. "Damn you, Gabe Stockman!" She trembled with indignant anger. "I asked because I was interested. I care about people."

"You have a hell of a way of showing it." He continued forward and picked up the last bale.

Jonni planted herself in his path. "Exactly what is that supposed to mean?"

Gabe stopped, resting much of the weight of the bale against his leg. "It means for the past six years you've been waltzing around New York in your fancy clothes and jewelry. You didn't have time for anyone but yourself. Then you get a notion to do a bit of slumming and turn up here. What are we supposed to do? Get down on our knees and be grateful a Kansas Starr has decided to come back to our heavens for two weeks?"

When he started to push his way by her, Jonni grabbed at his forearm to stop him. "I couldn't come back before now. I was working."

"Sure." His tone was derisive.

"I was working!" she repeated angrily.

"Very hard work it was, too," Gabe mocked. "Getting your picture taken."

"It sounds easy, does it?" Jonni snapped. "You should try it sometime. Get up at the crack of dawn and rush to some studio. Sit in a chair for two hours to have your makeup done and your hair styled. Then pose in front of hot, bright lights for hours and smile until the muscles in your cheeks quiver and ache. Some designer is usually standing in the background screaming that you're perspiring all over his magnificent creation. Oh, I have an absolute ball every minute, Gabe!"

"It sounds like it," he commented, some of the coldness leaving his look.

"It doesn't end when the camera is out of film," Jonni continued, still steaming from his previous remark. "No, you have to watch what you eat so you don't gain weight or so your face doesn't break out in unsightly blemishes. And you have to go to bed early so the camera won't discover any shadows under your eyes the next day. It's a very glamorous profession, but not when you're in it. It's work, hot, tiring work. If you want to stay on top, you have to fight for every assignment, the way I've had to the past six years." Her voice rang with six years of tiredness, frustration and disillusionment.

Sensing that the heat of her temper had been vented, Gabe stepped around her with the bale and walked down the row, speaking as he walked. "I told you six years ago you wouldn't like it. That kind of life isn't for you. But you wouldn't listen to me."

"Is that what all this has been leading up to?" Jonni asked with open-mouthed incredulity. "You just wanted an opportunity to say 'I told you so,' didn't you? You're forgetting that when you tried to talk me out of going six years ago, you also told me I wouldn't make it. Well, I didn't fail, Gabe. I'm the best in the business." She was stating facts, not bragging.

"So?" He dropped the bale and reached down to snap the twine. "Is that why you stuck it out even after you discovered you didn't like it?"

"Partly," she admitted. "You were so positive I was going to fall flat on my face that I was determined to prove you were wrong."

Gabe straightened, drawing his head back to study her and gauge the truth of her statement. "Okay, so you've proved that. Now what? Since it hasn't turned out to be the bed of roses you envisaged and you don't like it, why go on with it after you're married?''

For an instant, Jonni faltered over the answer. "It isn't that many more years before I'll be too old. It's rare for someone over thirty to decorate a magazine cover. Trevor and I have discussed it and decided that it's only logical for me to continue while I'm still in demand," she reasoned.

"Was that your decision? Or Trevor's?" A dark brow lifted in silent challenge.

"Ours," she retorted. "Besides, what else would I do?"

"Be a wife and mother."

"My God, is that old-fashioned!" She laughed scornfully at his answer. "You're out of step with the times, Gabe."

"Am I?" he countered. "I thought that's what women's liberation was all about—to give women a choice of whether they wanted to work or stay at home without any stigma being attached to either." He picked up the loose hay and began distributing it in the mangers of the remaining stalls. "By the way, where's lover boy this morning?" His voice was dryly sardonic in its reference to Trevor.

Simmering, Jonni took a deep breath and made a rapid mental count to ten. "If you mean Trevor, he's still in bed, sleeping." At Gabe's brief, derisive glance, she found herself rushing to defend Trevor's sleeping habits and was irritated. "Trevor rarely goes to bed before midnight, so he's accustomed to sleeping late."

"That's some marriage you're going to have," Gabe scoffed. All the horses were now munching at their hay. Finished, Gabe walked toward the open barn door, removing his gloves as he went.

"You get up with the sun and he sleeps late. He stays up until all hours of the night and you go to bed early. About the only time you'll be able to spend with each other is over the dinner table," he concluded as they emerged into the morning sunshine.

Slightly stunned, Jonni realized that she had never looked at their differing habits in quite that light before. It left her feeling a little shaken, but she glossed over it.

"I'm sure we can arrange our schedules so we can spend time together." But she was wondering how.

"Marriage by appointment," Gabe mocked. Dinner at 7:00 P.M., make love at 8:00 P.M. At 9:00 P.M., wife goes to sleep, husband leaves bedroom."

Phrased that way, it sounded very cold-blooded. It irritated Jonni that Gabe had pointed out a problem she should have considered, and for which she should already have found a more adequate solution than the callous one he had offered.

"What is it about Trevor that you don't like?" she demanded impatiently. As Gabe veered away from her Jonni added another sharp question. "Where are you going?"

"My truck is parked near the pond by the other barn," he said, without breaking stride.

Her long legs continued to follow him. "I don't

even know why I asked you about Trevor," she grumbled. "You've found fault with everyone I've dated."

"I don't see that it matters whether or not I like him," Gabe pointed out. "You're the one who's going to marry him."

"It doesn't matter," she insisted.

Ahead of them was the pickup truck, Gabe continued toward it, tapping the leather gloves in his hand against the side of his leg as he walked. The sound picked at Jonni's nerves, stretched as taut as banjo strings.

CHAPTER FIVE

"THE POND IS LOW," Jonni observed.

She stood on the knoll overlooking the man-made catch basin. The truck was parked on the other side of Gabe. An earthen dam had been built across a natural hollow in the land to trap the runoff of melting snows and spring rains, to insure water for the livestock through the long summer. A two-foot-wide ring of mud encircled the water. A duck waddled across the slowly drying band toward the encroaching grass.

"The wind blew away what little snowfall we had last winter. So far it's been a dry spring with barely enough rain to get the ground wet," Gabe explained, and Jonni recalled her father's similar comment last night. "Another week of this and everything around here is going to be as dry as a tinderbox. Even the Cimarron is low."

Jonni heard the morning breeze rustling through the grass, a dry sound. She was a rancher's daughter; she knew what a drought could mean. She watched Gabe remove his hat and comb his fingers through the thickness of his dark hair. It was a troubled gesture. He turned slightly to study the sky to the south as if hoping to see moisture-laden clouds coming up from the Gulf, graying the horizon.

There wasn't a cloud in sight, not even a puffy marshmallow one. The creases around his eyes deepened as he squinted into the sun. Sighing, Gabe looked away and settled the wide-brimmed hat firmly on his head.

"I've got to be going," he said. "With no rain to stimulate new growth, the grazing isn't good. We're moving the cattle again today—this time to the river pasture." His mouth quirked. "The boys are waiting for me and, as usual, you've held me up."

"Yes." Jonni smiled at the remark. "You were always telling me I was keeping you from your work," she remembered. "You used to say if I wanted to talk to you, I had to do it while you were working. And you usually made me help."

"You were in better condition then. An eighty-pound bale would have been heavy, but you'd have been able to lift it." A hint of a smile softened his mouth.

Suddenly everything seemed all right again. Their sharp bickering a few moments ago was forgotten as a warm, beaming smile spread across Jonni's face.

"It's good to be home again," she said. "It's wonderful to breathe fresh air again and be surrounded by a wide-open sky. I won't have to worry about how I look." She laughed. "I don't even have to put on makeup if I don't want to. It will be a glorious two weeks—riding wherever I want to and as far as I want to." There was a faintly wistful look in her blue eyes. "I wish I could go with you to move the cattle. It would be like old times."

"Why don't you come?" His low-pitched drawl extended a persuasive invitation. Jonni glanced uncertainly in the direction of the house, hidden from view by the barn. The curve of Gabe's mouth became twisted. "I forgot—you'll want to be here when lover boy gets up."

Turning to face him, Jonni forgot to take offense at his remark. They weren't standing that far apart. Something Trevor had said about him the day before make her look at Gabe as a man and not someone she had known for years.

She was tall, but Gabe was taller. Well-muscled, he was a very virile man with a frankly sexual way of looking at a woman. There was a fluttering in the pit of her stomach. She guessed he affected a lot of women that way. She discovered an unexpected curiosity about his personal life.

"Why haven't you ever married, Gabe?" she asked, tipping her head to one side. "Haven't you ever thought about it?"

"Yeah, I thought about it seriously, once," he acknowledged, but Jonni had the impression of a door slamming in his expression, shutting her out of his inner thoughts.

"What happened?" she persisted.

"It didn't work out," was all he said.

Jonni wanted a more specific answer, but the squawking of a duck diverted her attention. A courting drake with his wings spread was approaching the duck that had just left the pond. The female was resisting his advances. The drake put up with her foolishness for only a few seconds before he began chasing her across the grass. The female immediately tried to escape him.

The two went running and flying over the ground, ducking under the board fence. Before they disappeared from sight behind a wooden feeder, Jonni saw the drake grab the duck's neck with his bill to force her to the ground. Jonni wasn't embarrassed by the ritual of animal breeding. On a ranch, procreation was necessary for livelihood, and accepted as the natural course of events in life—all life.

Gabe, who had observed the primitive courtship scene as well, turned to look at her. "You came home just in time for the mating season." The bold look in his eyes disturbed the normal rhythm of her pulse.

"It seems I did," Jonni agreed with a half smile, refusing to be self-conscious about the facts of life.

"I wonder—" there was an undercurrent of intensity in his drawling voice, a darkening of his gaze "—whether Trevor has ever grabbed you by the neck...like this." He raised his arm, and before Jonni could take a step backward, his hand had imprisoned the back of her neck in a viselike grip. Shocked by the quality of ruthlessness about him, Jonni strained against his hold, her hands pushing at his chest, but not a sound came from her paralyzed throat.

"Or pulled you into his arms—" Gabe continued in the same deadly tone "—like this." Her stunned resistance offered no more of an obstacle to him than a toothpick attempting to ward off an encircling band of iron as he gathered her to him. Her head was tipped back to stare at him in mute astonishment. Alarm quivered through her nerve ends as his black mustache moved closer. "Or kissed you. . . ."

Despite the pause, he didn't add the words "like this" to the sentence. Instead his mouth covered her lips, claiming them in a hard kiss of possession. The suede material of his vest was sensually rough beneath the palms of her hands, like the soft brush of his mustache against her skin.

All sorts of reactions were being aroused by the driving power of his mouth, which demanded a response. His embrace lacked the practiced technique and expertise she had come to expect from Trevor. Gabe's was simpler, more basic, awakening her flesh to the desire of all life forms to mate with the opposite sex.

The knowledge spread through her like a flame, heating her flesh wherever it was crushed to his masculine frame. Jonni trembled at the force of such a basic need, which could make her lips yield willingly to his compelling kiss when she would soon belong to another man.

The pressure of his mouth eased slowly, then it was taken away altogether as Gabe drew his head back. There was a disturbed heaviness to his breath, warm and caressing against her skin. Her eyes opened slowly, mirroring the shock of her discovery. Something hardened in his expression. His arms loosened their hold until her legs were no longer resting against the support of his hard thighs.

Bewildered by her reaction, Jonni raised her left hand to her lips as if by touching them she might discover the cause. His eyes narrowed at the gesture, his arms returning to his side.

"Why did you do that, Gabe?" She had experienced passion before, but this had gone beyond that to something more profound.

The sun touched her diamond and flashed a prism of light onto the shadowed features below the hat brim. Gabe looked grim.

"How the hell do I know?" he muttered thickly. "What eats at me is I should have done it six years ago."

While Jonni was still puzzling over his cryptic response, Gabe pivoted and took long, swift strides to the parked truck. Her left hand reached out toward his departing figure, the words forming on her lips to call him back and explain it. Then she saw the engagement ring on her finger. Suddenly she didn't want to know if what she suspected he was saying was really true. That shaky feeling inside her made her afraid of his answer.

No, don't ask him to explain, she told herself as he gunned the motor of the pickup and reversed away from the pond. The wisest thing to do would be to forget about the kiss. She was engaged to Trevor and there wouldn't be a repeat. But she wished she could quit shaking. Shoving her hands in her pockets, she decided to walk it off.

It was an hour later when she made her way back to the house. Trevor was just coming down the stairs when she entered. The large grandfather clock in the foyer struck nine. One look told Jonni that Trevor had showered as well as shaved.

Dressed more casually this morning, he wore dark blue trousers, a white turtleneck and a blue and gray tweed jacket with decorative leather patches at the elbows.

"Good morning." She assumed a bright smile as she greeted him. "You're up early this morning." She repeated the phrase she herself had had addressed to her.

"Good morning," he returned, and bent to kiss her.

For some inexplicable reason, Jonni offered him her cheek. Trevor didn't force a more intimate exchange. She wondered why she'd done it. Guilt, perhaps? Did she think Trevor would be able to taste Gabe's kiss on her lips? Damn, she was supposed to forget about that. But Trevor didn't seem to observe that she was behaving out of the ordinary.

"After years of being lulled to sleep by the blare of horns and the sounds of traffic, would you believe that the sound of a motor woke me up?" He smiled in wry amusement.

Jonni remembered Gabe's noisy, wheel-spinning departure in the pickup and tried to join in Trevor's amusement at the irony of his statement.

"Who was it? Do you know?" he asked with absent interest.

"It was Gabe," she admitted. "He was on his way out to help move the cattle to another pasture."

"He was probably loud deliberately," Trevor mused.

"If he was, I'm glad," Jonni teased. "It's time you were getting up. I hope you had a good night's sleep, though. Was the bed comfortable?"

He linked his hands behind her waist, drawing her hips against his. "I can think of ways it could have been more comfortable." He nuzzled her cheek.

"But yes, I had a good night after I became used to the frogs croaking and the owls hooting. Mother Nature is very noisy," he concluded, taking a tiny nibble at her earlobe.

"You were listening to her night music." Jonni smiled. The sounds had been very soothing to her.

"It was monotonously loud. You should file a complaint and have her turn the volume down," Trevor mocked, and Jonni laughed softly at his silly suggestion. "Don't you think she would listen?"

"No, I don't." She lifted her gaze from its study of his rolled collar, amusement twinkling in her eyes.

His expression became serious. "Have I told you yet this morning that I love you, Jonni Starr?"

"No." She shook her head.

His mouth made the pledge as he covered her lips with a possessive kiss. Jonni responded to it and fought aside a comparison with Gabe's kiss. The result was as pleasant and satisfying as always. There was a curve to her mouth when they drew apart.

"Mmm, that was nice," she murmured.

"It merely whetted my appetite," he assured her.

"That's because you haven't had breakfast," Jonni teased.

His hands moved caressingly along her waist and hips. "I know what I'd like." His gaze roamed suggestively over her and stopped at a spot near her left shoulder. "What's this?" Trevor plucked a piece of hay from the knitted weave of her sweater. "What have you been doing this morning? Rolling in the hay?"

"No," Jonni denied with a self-conscious laugh. "I was at the barn, helping Gabe give the horses some hay."

"So that's what I smell."

"I was just coming in to wash," she assured him.

"Why don't you change, too?" Trevor suggested, his gaze raking her figure. "What you're wearing doesn't do anything for you. Don't you have something more attractive to put on?"

"Of course," Jonni admitted, and started to explain that she hadn't felt like wearing any of her more stylish pantsuits.

"Good," Trevor interrupted. "I want you to look beautiful for me."

Jonni hesitated for only an instant before nodding an agreement. He wasn't asking that much. It seemed churlish to refuse. "Mom and dad might still be in the kitchen. If not, the coffee is on the stove. Help yourself and I'll be down in a few minutes," she promised as she slipped out of his arms to climb the stairs.

In her bedroom she paused in front of the mirror. The jeans and sweater didn't look that unat-

tractive on her. In fact, Jonni thought the denims
showed her slim, leggy look, and the sweater
rounded out nicely over her breasts to nip in at her
waistline. But the clothes were a bit shabby and
worn, which was probably Trevor's objection.

Stripping out of them, she chose a pair of camel
tan slacks and a matching vest to go with her white
blouse. The tan color accented her hair, the faded
dark gold of an antique painting. After applying a
touch of makeup, Jonni turned downstairs to join
Trevor and her parents.

THE DISHES FROM THE EVENING MEAL had been
washed and put away. Jonni sat in the living room
feeling restless and on edge, as if the walls were
closing in on her. Caroline had just taken the coffee service back to the kitchen. Gabe had disappeared immediately after dinner with the excuse
that there was paperwork to be done. A silence
was gaping between her father and Trevor. Jonni
slipped her hand into the grasp of Trevor's.

"Let's go out on the porch for a while," she
suggested.

"Some fresh air sounds good," Trevor agreed,
but glanced to her father.

"You two go ahead." John waved a hand.
"You don't need my permission."

Rising together, they walked to the front door.
As Trevor opened it, Jonni heard her mother
return to the living room.

"Where did Jonni and Trevor go?" she asked
John.

"Outside."

"Oh, but I wanted to show Jonni...." her mother began in disgruntled protest.

"They want to be alone for a little while, Caroline," her father interrupted. "Or have you forgotten what it was like to be in love and engaged?"

Jonni didn't hear her mother's answer as Trevor ushered her outside and closed the door. His arm curved around her waist and they strolled to the far end of the porch. The sun had gone down more than an hour earlier and the night was dark.

"I didn't realize the night could be so black," Trevor commented.

"That's because you're used to streetlights and neon signs," Jonni told him.

Except for a quarter moon hanging in the sky, a light shining from the window of Gabe's quarters and the lights from the house, there wasn't any illumination. Not even the stars had lighted their twinkling fires.

An owl hooted in the trees. A chorus of frogs sang at the pond, a sound muted by the evening breeze whispering through the grass. From far off in the night, Jonni heard the bellowing of a bull.

"It's the mating season," she recalled, and a shiver danced over her skin.

Trevor leaned his back against a supporting column of the porch roof. His arms circled around her to draw her shoulders against his chest. It was warm in his arms and she nestled closer, letting her head rest against his cheekbone. He crossed his arms in front of her stomach.

"That's a fine thing to say," he murmured near her ear, "when you know your parents are just inside the house." His hand slid inside her vest to cover her breast.

Turning her face toward his mouth, Jonni smiled as he found the corner of her lips. She hadn't meant to sound provocative, but now his embrace was conjuring up memories that were more disturbing.

"Why are you smiling?" Trevor asked, amused and curious.

I was remembering other times when I was on this porch," she explained.

"In somebody else's arms?" he quizzed.

"Yes, until daddy turned the porch light on." Her smile widened. "It was a very unsubtle hint that I'd been out here an improper length of time and I should come in."

"At least with you, he knows your intentions are honorable." She turned in his arms, sliding her hands around his neck.

He kissed her once, twice, then drew back. "As much as I'm tempted to indulge in a front-porch necking scene, I don't feel like taking a cold shower later on," he said firmly.

With a sigh that bordered on disappointment at his control, Jonni half turned in his arms to rest a shoulder against his chest and cuddle into his tweed jacket for warmth. A frown knitted her forehead and she forced it away. She had been feigning passion and now she was irritated with Trevor for not responding. What was the matter with her?

She tried changing the subject. "Mother asked me if we would like to go to church with them in the morning."

"I suppose it's expected?" His inflection made it a question.

"Yes."

"Then I'd be delighted to go," he mocked.

"I'll tell her," she promised. After another few seconds had passed she said, "I thought I might go riding for a while tomorrow afternoon. Would you like to come along?"

"My love, you know I don't like horses," Trevor reminded her. "Since I can't persuade you to stay away from them, don't try to persuade me to get on one."

"All right," she sighed.

"How on earth are you going to keep from being bored to death during these next two weeks?" he asked suddenly, sounding genuinely perplexed. "There's nothing to do around here, and you're miles from civilization."

"Miles from civilization?" Jonni laughed at his words. "I'll have you know, Trevor Alexander Martin the Third, that this ranch has indoor plumbing, the very latest kitchen equipment, an entire range of entertainment from stereo to television and radio, a pool table and billiard table, an extensive library, a garden to putter in, horses to ride and an endless array of breathtaking landscapes to view. Every type of amusement is right at hand. We don't have to go anywhere."

"I'll take Broadway and Carnegie Hall any day," Trevor responded, unimpressed by her list.

"I would have added a swimming hole except the pond is too low." Jonni searched the cloudless night sky. "I hope it rains soon."

"My God!" He released a derisive, laughing

breath. "Now you're beginning to sound like your father and Gabe at dinner tonight!"

"The lack of water is serious," Jonni insisted with a thread of impatience at his lack of understanding for the critical situation the range was in.

"I'm sure it is," he agreed in a placating tone. "But it hardly concerns us, does it?"

Jonni swallowed the sharp retort that trembled on her tongue. "No, I guess not," she agreed to avoid an argument, and sighed again.

"It's past your bedtime, isn't it?" Trevor straightened from the post and shifted her out of his arms. "You'd better go in so you can get your beauty sleep."

She didn't feel tired, but she didn't feel like continuing this conversation, either. "It's been a long day," she offered by way of agreement. She took a step toward the door, then looked back over her shoulder at him. "Are you coming in?"

"Not right away."

"Good night," she wished him.

"Good night," he returned.

THE NEXT MORNING Jonni was standing in church between Trevor and Gabe, singing from the hymnal and listening to Trevor's resonant baritone voice. It carried above the voices of the rest of the congregation. Only one voice competed with his natural volume, and it belonged to the stoop-shouldered woman in the row ahead of them. Unfortunately her wavering voice was way off-key. When she hit a sharply discordant note, Jonni saw Trevor wince. Jonni tried hard not to smile.

When the last note of the organ had echoed
through the rafters the congregation sat and
turned to the pages of the responsive reading.
Trevor leaned sideways toward her.

"Someone should tell that poor woman she
can't sing," he whispered in a censorious tone.

"That woman happens to be my great-aunt
Maude and she's practically stone deaf," Jonni
whispered back. "She can hardly hear herself, let
alone the organ."

Gabe's attention didn't waver from the book he
held as he added his low comment to their conversation. "The Bible says to make 'joyful noise unto
the Lord.' It doesn't say the noise has to be in
tune."

Jonni thought his dryly forgiving remark was
amusing, but Trevor didn't. He glared across her
at Gabe's partially bowed head as he studied the
pages of the book. Jonni struggled to keep a
straight face and finally succeeded. As the minister
began the responsive reading she stole a glance at
Gabe. A complacent gleam lighted his dark eyes
but he continued to look to the front of the church
at the pulpit.

Hatless in God's house, his dark hair sprang
thickly in a careless, vital style. He wore a
Western-cut suit of brown with a plain bronze tie.
He looked comfortable and at ease. Jonni had difficulty assimilating the fact that he was the same
man who had disturbed her with his kiss less than
twenty-four hours ago. He certainly had been ignoring her since then. Not ignoring her, she corrected, but just treating her very casually.

His attention shifted and Gabe caught her staring at him. He lifted a dark eyebrow in a silent question, as if he had no idea what she might be thinking about. Jonni looked swiftly away, dragging her concentration back to the church service.

When it was over and the benediction said, the exodus from church began. Jonni knew practically everyone who had attended. Since she was a hometown girl who had become something of a celebrity, everyone wanted to speak to her. Her mother had already begun spreading the word that she had become engaged, so naturally everyone wanted to meet Trevor, as well. They all seemed to cluster on the church lawn, and few cars left the lot. At some point Jonni became separated from Trevor, and as she turned to see where he was, her mother came over to her.

"Your Aunt Maude is standing over by the steps. You'd better go over and say hello to her," she suggested.

"All right, mother," Jonni agreed, and asked, "have you seen Trevor?"

"He's over there with your father and Jack Sloane."

Jonni looked in the direction her mother pointed. Trevor looked up, saw her and shrugged in a helpless gesture, indicating he was trapped for a few polite minutes. She smiled and made her way through the crowd to the church steps where the aging woman stood, leaning on her cane to catch her breath.

"Hello, Aunt Maude." Jonni greeted the woman in a loud voice as she stopped in front of her.

The woman was in her eighties, yellow gray hair thinning away from her wrinkled face. "Do you remember me?"

"What did you say?" Frowning, Maude Starr turned her head for Jonni to repeat what she asked in her good ear. "Speak up."

"I said—" Jonni leaned closer and spoke louder "— it's me, Jonni."

"Of course it's you," the woman snapped. "Do you think I'm blind?"

After six years, her great-aunt was still an irascible old grouch, Jonni discovered. She tried not to smile. "How are you?"

"What did you say?" Again her forehead acquired extra creases. "You'll have to speak up, girl. My hearing isn't very good."

"I said, how are you?" Jonni repeated.

"You don't have to shout! I'm fine, fine." A palsied hand shifted the cane to a more supportive position. "Sybil Crane told me you're getting married. Is that true?"

"Yes," Jonni admitted with an exaggerated bobbing of her head so the positive answer would be understood.

"Well, where is this young man of yours? Aren't you going to introduce me to him?" her aunt demanded in a querulous voice.

"He's standing over there." Jonni made the mistake of turning her head to point out Trevor.

"What? How many times do I have to tell you to speak up?" A pair of sharp blue eyes sparkled with impatience.

Jonni breathed in to contain her exasperation

over the conversation and maintained a pleasant expression. This time she didn't make the mistake of turning as she spoke. "He's right over there."

The woman's gaze followed her pointing arm, then snapped back to Jonni. "Why didn't you say you were marrying him?" she sniffed. "Did you think because my hearing is fading that my memory is, too? Gabe Stockman has been working at your father's ranch for a good many years now. Didn't you think I'd remember that?"

Gabe Stockman? Jonni's head swiveled to see Gabe walking toward them, directly in line with her pointing finger and blocking out Trevor from view. "No, you don't understand, Aunt Maude." She hurried to correct the mistake. "I'm not engaged to him."

"Of course you've got engaged to him. Do you think I don't know what we're talking about? My mind hasn't wandered anywhere, although I'm beginning to worry about yours."

Aunt Maude jabbed a gnarled, arthritic finger toward Jonni in accusation. A flowered handkerchief, tucked under the expansion band of her wristwatch, fluttered below the finger.

"No, Aunt Maude, there's been a mistake," Jonni insisted, trying not to lose her patience.

"Nobody wants to make a mistake when they choose a man to marry," her aunt declared, catching only part of what was said, and Jonni wanted to scream in frustration. How on earth was she going to make the woman understand? To make the situation worse, Gabe arrived to stand beside her. The older woman cast an approving glance at him before addressing Jonni. "You couldn't have picked a better man. Gabe here will make you a good husband."

Jonni didn't quite meet the questioning and amused look he sent her. "I've been talking myself hoarse trying to convince Aunt Maude that I was pointing Trevor as the man I was going to marry, not you," she explained, her voice pitched to a quiet level.

Maude Starr saw her lips moving and cupped a hand to her good ear. "What did you say? I can't hear you if you don't speak up." Her brow furrowed in a deep frown.

"I was..." Jonni began at a louder volume.

Gabe bent forward to shout in the woman's good ear. "She was talking to me, Maude. How are you today?"

"Fine, fine." A palsied hand waved aside the question. "That engagement ring you gave Jonni is too gaudy," she criticized. "It's in bad taste. You should take it back for something smaller."

"I'll think about that." He nodded as if taking the matter under consideration.

"Jonni is a good girl. You be sure and treat her right, Gabe Stockman."

Jonni was fuming at his failure to correct her aunt's misconception. "Will you please explain to her?" she ordered through clenched teeth, her lips barely moving.

When Gabe glanced at her, there was a dangerous glint in his dark eyes, wicked and dancing. Her pulse fluttered. Again he bent closer to the old woman to speak loudly in her ear.

"You know what they say about breaking in a new horse—a cowboy has to ride it hard and long in the beginning if he wants it to be worth a damn later on."

Her mouth opened, but Jonni didn't know whether to rage at him in angry frustration or simply hit him. Maude drew her head back, looking properly shocked by his innuendo, but it was Jonni she turned on, shaking her finger.

"You'd better teach him some manners," she informed Jonni in no uncertain terms. "In my day, a man didn't speak of such things in female company." With that, Maude moved away from them, tottering on her cane.

Recovering from her initial speechlessness, Jonni glared at Gabe and demanded, "Why did you do that?"

"I thought you needed rescuing," he answered evenly. The glint in his eyes was still there, but for the most part it was veiled.

"What I needed was for you to explain to Maude that you and I aren't getting married," she retorted.

"She would have asked endless questions and it would have taken the better part of the day to straighten her out," Gabe reasoned.

"So you let her go on thinking we're engaged," Jonni reminded him. "That wasn't right."

Someone else will explain it to her," he said, completely untroubled.

It was true, but Jonni wasn't about to stop berating him. "And how could you make such an off-color remark to her? That was unforgivable!

She's a spinster. You know she's never been married.''

"Who knows? She might have some of the best dreams she's had in months," Gabe drawled, openly mocking Jonni's indignant air. "Besides, a person can't live to be her age without learning all there is to know about life. She pretended to be shocked for your benefit."

"You're impossible!" Jonni declared in an angry breath.

"So I've been told," he smiled.

She saw Trevor approaching and hurried to meet him.

CHAPTER SIX

AFTER SUNDAY DINNER Jonni went upstairs to her room and changed into her riding clothes. On her way down she met Trevor coming up. They paused midway on the staircase.

"I'm going out riding for an hour or so," she told him. "Are you sure you wouldn't like to come along?" The question was asked more out of politeness than in the hope he might reconsider.

"No, thank you." Trevor made the anticipated refusal. "I'm going upstairs to change. Afterward I intend to become entrenched in the newspaper."

"Ah, the newspaper, a touch of civilization in this wilderness," Jonni teased him.

"Precisely, my love." He kissed her lightly on the mouth. "Enjoy yourself."

"I will."

Jonni continued down the steps, then walked at an unhurried pace out the door and down the path toward the barn. It was another clear, sunny day, the temperature pleasantly cool, a good day for riding.

The tack-room door stood open. Gabe was inside, removing the broken chin strap from a bridle.

He had changed out of his suit into a white shirt

and a pair of mud-colored denims. He glanced up when Jonni entered then resumed his repair of the bridle.

"I'm going riding," Jonni announced. "Would you like to suggest a horse or should I take my choice?" She was curt, resentment still smoldering from the incident with her aunt at the church.

"A pleasure ride?" Gabe glanced up again to see her affirmative nod. "Take Sancho, the zebra dun in the first stall. You can use the saddle and bridle there, on your left."

As Jonni reached for the bridle and saddle blanket, he added, "If your fiancé needs a gentle mount, you can saddle the claybank mare for him. She's as placid as they come."

"Trevor isn't going riding." She slipped her arm through the bridle's headstall to drape it on her shoulder.

"I forgot. He's a city dude. He probably doesn't know how to ride, does he?" Gabe pitched the broken chin strap into the trash barrel. His action seemed to indicate he thought Trevor deserved the same treatment.

"As a matter of fact, Trevor can ride very well. He just doesn't like horses, nor does he enjoy riding them. So it isn't likely it would be something he'd do for pleasure."

As she issued the information, Jonni was tautly aware of his eyes on her, following her every movement.

"When does he ride, then?" he challenged in skepticism.

"One of his investors from Virginia does a lot of

fox hunting. I know Trevor has ridden with him on several occasions.''

She gathered up the blanket and saddle pad. She felt on edge and blamed it on Gabe's inquisition, which seemed an attempt to find fault with Trevor.

"In other words, he goes riding when there's money involved, but not for the pleasure of being with you.'' Gabe succeeded in coming up with a conclusion that made Trevor look bad.

"I wouldn't want him doing it *just* for me,'' Jonni retorted.

There was a pause and Jonni thought she had finally silenced him. But she hadn't. "You're a morning person. Trevor prefers the night. You like riding horses. He doesn't. Do the two of you have anything in common?'' Gabe taunted.

Gripping the handhold behind the saddle horn, she lifted the saddle to the back of her shoulder. "Yes,'' she snapped out the answer. "We happen to love each other.''

While she still had the last word, Jonni stalked out of the tack room. The dun gelding turned its head to look at her as she entered its stall. She slapped its flank to move it over. With an economy of motion, she set the saddle and blankets down and walked to its head to slip the bridle on over the horse's halter.

Although Jonni half expected it, Gabe didn't follow her out of the tack room to pursue the conversation. Once the horse was saddled, she led it out of the stall and out the side door. Looping the reins around its neck, she stepped into a stirrup and swung into the saddle. With a turn of the reins she pointed the zebra dun toward open land and touched her heels to its belly. Its first stride carried it into a canter.

Jonni's tension eased as she widened the distance to the barn. A mile from the headquarters of the ranch, she stroked the tan gray neck and slowed the gelding to a reaching trot. Tossing its black mane, the horse emitted a rolling snort. It was a contented, relaxed sound, which Jonni echoed with a sigh.

The land she rode through was wild and untamed. Its rocky, uneven terrain defied the rancher's attempts to subdue it, tolerating only the tenacious grasses, which drove hardy roots into the soil. The horizon was marked by jutting mesas and towering buttes. Their shapes had been created by wind and erosion carving into the red-stained sandstone and shale.

It was with regret that Jonni turned her mount toward the ranch before her hour was up. She would have ridden longer and farther if Trevor hadn't been waiting at the house for her to return. But there would be other days during the next two weeks when she could ride and Trevor would be in New York. There would be plenty of time to indulge in the luxury of riding without being confined by the boundaries of riding paths in a city park.

Jonni reached the corral gate, opened it, rode through and maneuvered the dun horse into position so she could close it. One horse was loose inside the enclosure, a bay gelding. Gabe was standing beside it, cradling its front hoof in his hand. Although her antagonism had faded on the ride, Jonni tried to ignore his presence.

"Did you have a good ride?" His conversational tone kept her from succeeding.

"Yes, I enjoyed it." It was impossible to keep the genuine sincerity out of her voice. She felt refreshed and glowing, and looked it. Gabe patted the bay's shoulder and walked away from it. The gelding limped heavily toward the barn. "He's lame. What happened?"

"He fell on the ice this winter and lacerated the tendon in his front knee." Gabe didn't look back at the horse as he walked to where Jonni had halted her mount. "It healed stiffly. Looks like he'll always have a game leg."

A permanently crippled horse on a working ranch, and a gelding at that—Jonni knew that spelled bad news. "Will he have to be destroyed?"

"The verdict isn't in yet. He's one of the cow horses we have on the place. We probably won't decide anything for sure until the fall. It isn't that easy to replace a horse like Joker," Gabe told her.

"No, I know it isn't," she agreed quietly. A horse could make a cowboy's job easier or harder. And a really good horse could almost work by itself.

Gabe stopped beside her horse and combed a wayward chunk of black mane onto the proper side of the horse's neck. In doing so, his gaze strayed beyond Jonni in the direction of the house. His look became dry and dusty.

"Speaking of jokers, there's your lover boy on the porch."

"Gabe, will you stop calling him that?" Jonni sighed impatiently and turned in her saddle to wave. Trevor wore charcoal gray slacks and an oyster-white sweater. It was a heavily ribbed knit, very rugged and manly. Trevor raised an acknowledging hand in response.

Standing in the stirrups, Jonni cupped her hands to her mouth to call, "I'll be up shortly." Nodding that he'd heard her, Trevor went back into the house.

"Have you ever seen him when he had a speck of dirt on him?" Gabe mused aloud, not really expecting an answer. "I can't help wondering if he sweats."

"You're just jealous," Jonni accused, but she was uncomfortably aware that she found a trace of humor in the question.

"Maybe I am." There was something remote about the good-natured smile he gave her. Swinging a foot out of the off stirrup, Jonni started to dismount, but Gabe's large hands slid under her tan vest to span her slender waist and set her on the ground in front of him. His hands retained a light hold on her waist.

"I expected you to go racing to the house to fall in Trevor's arms, after being separated from him for more than an hour."

He was teasing her—in an old, familiar way that Jonni didn't find offensive. She was conscious of his hands on her waist. She could feel the outline of each finger through the material of her blouse as if he was touching her bare skin. His touch was warm and oddly stimulating. Her forearms were resting on his, her hands feeling the muscled flesh beneath his sleeves.

She laughed, trying to ignore how closely she stood to him. "I wouldn't throw myself in Trevor's arms," she denied. "Not when I'm smelling like a horse." Raising a hand, she sniffed at it and wrinkled her nose in distaste, laughing softly.

Gabe captured the same hand by the wrist and carried it so close to his face that Jonni could feel the tickling brush of his mustache against her fingers. Her breathing became shallow as she lifted her gaze to meet the growing darkness of his.

"You smell good to me," he said quietly. "Earthy and fresh like the land after a spring rain."

Jonni didn't draw her hand out of his grasp. She knew she should have. Her heartbeat began to quicken as his gaze slid to her mouth. He was going to kiss her, and she realized that she wanted him to. The pressure on her waist increased to draw her forward, but she was drifting that way, swept along by a powerful undercurrent she was powerless to resist.

There was no haste to achieve the union of their lips as their bodies slowly fitted together perfectly. His breath caressed her skin and Jonni inhaled the heady male aroma that belonged distinctly to him. When the kiss came, it was gentle and deep. It evoked a response from her that was more ravishing and seductive than hard passion. It was a bright, burning flame that curled all the way down to her toes.

His mouth moved over hers as though he worshipped the shape and taste of it. His hand encircled her throat to caress the sensitive skin of her neck and finally he curved his fingers into her hair as his kiss became hungry in its adoration. Her parted lips were giving him every invitation to satisfy his appetite. The world seemed to be dissolving into a mist from the heat created by their two fusing bodies.

The caress of his hand at the base of her spine was sensually erotic, pressing her hips to the unyielding hardness of him. Jonni needed no encouragement to arch closer to the sexual radiance of his embrace. His caress blinded her to all but the sign language of desire, interpreting it to a degree she had never known before. His touch opened her heart to a piercing beauty that left Jonni shaken with alarm. She was trembling from it when his mouth trailed langorously to her temple. The black velvet hair above his lips tangled with her windswept curls.

During the kiss she had fitted herself to him like a skintight glove. Now the first chilling winds of reality began to steal in. Lowering her head, Jonni stared at the buttons on his shirt and the shadow of chest hair beneath the white material. Her arms uncurled from around his neck to wedge a small space between their bodies. She suddenly realized why the perfection of their embrace had been wrong. The problem could be summed up in one word—Trevor.

When she lifted her wary and bewildered gaze to his face, his dark eyes were waiting to meet it. They studied her expression intently, while his features betrayed nothing of his inner thoughts.

"Well?" Gabe prompted. He was aware of her emotional withdrawal, but was making no effort to reverse it.

"You'd better not do this anymore." It wasn't a warning, a statement or a plea, but a combination of all three.

There was a complacent twist to his mouth as he said, "You'd better not let me." The low drawl held the faintest hint of mockery. In the next second he let her go and turned to gather the trailing reins. "I'll take care of your horse for you."

Heat scorched her cheeks as Jonni watched him lead the dun gelding to the barn. She hadn't offered a word in her own defense because she knew Gabe was right. There had been no coercion in the embrace. She had been willing and eager for the kiss, a ready participant. And it had been enormously satisfying.

Now she had to go to the house, where Trevor waited. The prospect didn't do much for her peace of mind. Try as she might, Jonni couldn't shrug off the kiss as innocent experimentation. In the first place Gabe wasn't the kind to experiment, and secondly, she was as guilty as he was for letting it happen.

Her homecoming was turning out to be nothing like she expected. In fact, her whole world seemed to be turning upside down. Jonni wasn't sure, yet, how she was going to put it right—the way it was before.

SHE HAD INTENDED to tell Trevor what had happened, to free her soul of the weight of guilt.

When the opportunity presented itself she had a severe case of cold feet. She rationalized her silence with the consolation that it had been a last fling. Bachelors did it all the time before that fateful wedding day. And, since she didn't expect Trevor to tell her all about his past affairs, there was no reason to speak to him of the indiscretions that happened before their marriage.

It all sounded very modern and independent, but her thoughts kept turning over and over to those few minutes in Gabe's arms. Each time she relived them she became more and more uneasy about them in her mind.

Her disturbed condition was intensified with each bounce of the pickup that rubbed her shoulder against Gabe's. The searing contact with his hard muscles was a physical reminder she didn't need. On a fairly smooth stretch of track, Jonni shifted to move closer to Trevor.

Ten minutes earlier the chartered aircraft had buzzed the house before entering the pattern to land at the ranch airfield. Trevor had finished his goodbyes to her parents. Gabe had already loaded the suitcases in the rear of the truck.

Against her better judgement, Jonni had ridden to the airstrip with them to say her final goodbye to Trevor.

The close confines of the truck's interior and the overwhelming force of Gabe's presence, as well as the freshness of memory, had kept her silent for much of the ride. Trevor noticed it, but he blamed it on his imminent departure. He wrapped an arm around her shoulders and kissed her hair.

"I'll call you every night," he assured her.

"Early, I promise, so I won't keep you or your parents up."

"Good. I'll look forward to your phone calls." Jonni couldn't respond to his caress, not with Gabe sitting there. Her gaze strayed to Gabe's mustached profile. He was staring resolutely ahead, seemingly oblivious to both of them.

"I'm glad you're spending these two weeks here with your parents." Trevor smiled against her hair. "There won't be anything else for you to do but miss me!"

The truck spurted over the last hump, giving Jonni the impression that Gabe had stepped on the gas. But only the two of them were aware of what the potential for entertainment was. Trevor was blinded by ignorance.

"And to start making plans for our wedding." Jonni didn't know why she added that. It had been meant for Gabe, but just why she was determined to remind him of her engaged state, she couldn't say. For someone who claimed to be unavailable, she had certainly acted available to him.

The chartered plane had taxied to the metal shed and it sat waiting, its motors still running. From here Trevor would fly to Kansas City to make his connections on a commercial airline to New York. Gabe stopped the truck on the clear side of the wing. He stayed in the driver's seat while Trevor climbed out and reached back to help Jonni.

The roar of the plane's engines made conversation impossible. Turbulent currents generated by the propellers tumbled Jonni's ash blond hair around her head as Jonni walked with Trevor to the rear of the truck for his luggage. Balancing the smaller case under one arm and carrying the other in the same hand, Trevor cupped the back of her head in his free hand and pulled her forward. He kissed her long and deep with sensual expertise. Striding toward the open door of the plane, he waved to her. Jonni saw his mouth form the word goodbye but she couldn't hear his voice above the noise of the engines.

Shortly after the door closed, the plane began taxiing toward the end of the grass runway. Jonni watched it from her position near the rear of the truck. With one hand, she tried to keep her hair from blowing in her face as the spinning wind from the propellers kicked up red dust.

As she watched the plane take off, she was haunted by the discovery that Trevor's kiss had seemed all technique with no emotion. Or maybe she was the one with no emotion. Had it only been three days ago that she had arrived, so happy, so confident, so secure? The plane wagged its wings in final goodbye as it soared into the blue Kansas sky.

"Beautiful blonde stands forlornly near the runway while plane carrying her lover wings out of sight. It's a very touching scene, but I think it's been done before," Gabe mocked. "You should be able to come up with something more original than that, Jonni."

Pivoting at the sound of his voice, Jonni saw him standing on the opposite side of the pickup. An arm rested nonchalantly against the cab as he gazed at her across the open sides of the truck. Her expression was wary and resentful. She held his gaze for a split second, but it was much too penetrating. Half turning, she broke the contact and walked toward the passenger door.

"Let's go back to the house," she said stiffly.

"That's exactly the destination I had in mind," Gabe replied in an ultradry voice and ducked his long frame inside the cab.

Jonni climbed in the passenger seat and slammed the door. The window was rolled down on her side and she hugged the door frame. The empty expanse of seat between them yawned an invitation to be filled.

She flicked a look at Gabe, who had made no attempt to start the engine. His black eyes were fixed on her, brilliant with ironic humor.

"Are you afraid of me?" he taunted.

"Petrified." Her response was sarcastic, to hide the tremor of her nerves. "This truck won't go anywhere unless you start it."

"I wouldn't have guessed." He turned the key in the ignition and the motor rumbled into life. Jonni turned her gaze out her window. The plane was now just a dark speck in the sky.

"What's wrong, Jonni?" Gabe's voice was low and dangerously intimate. "Are you beginning to have second thoughts?"

"Yes...I mean, no." In her haste to answer, she stumbled over her words. A throaty laugh came from Gabe as he shifted into first gear. The sound scraped a raw nerve. "Would you like to tell me what's so damned funny?"

"You are." He slid a lazy, amused look her way

and let it roam insolently over her face. "You didn't have enough guts to tell lover boy about our little interlude and now you're eaten up with guilt."

A flame shot through her veins. The way he was looking at her made her realize he was making love to her in his mind, and her senses were quivering in response. It was crazy! She jerked her gaze from his face.

"You don't know that," she insisted. "Maybe I told him."

"I know *you*, Jonni. Don't forget that," Gabe warned. "There were too many times in the past when you brought your confessions to me. I recognize that look of trouble all locked up inside."

"Nothing is troubling me," Jonni lied stubbornly and turned cool blue eyes toward him.

"Like hell," he jeered, then shrugged. "But have it your way. You always do, anyway." The last sentence was offered in a bitter, grudging tone.

They bumped over the track to the house. After they had gone several hundred yards in silence, Jonni gave in to a compelling demand to obtain explanations.

"Gabe, I want to ask you a question," she said.

"Shoot." His gaze didn't leave the road.

"Why did you kiss me?"

He reached up and adjusted the mirror in the top center of the windshield, turning it so Jonni saw her reflection on its surface. "You're a beautiful woman, Jonni. Why wouldn't I want to kiss you?" Gabe answered with a question.

Releasing a quiet sigh, she turned to stare out the window. It wasn't a satisfactory answer, but maybe she had put the question to the wrong party. Maybe she should ask herself why she kissed him.

But she didn't. And she was relieved that Gabe didn't, either.

CHAPTER SEVEN

MONDAY AND TUESDAY slipped by with relative ease. With the extensive holdings of the Starr Ranch, there were many demands to occupy Gabe's time from sunup to sundown. As long as she wasn't in his company, Jonni could almost make believe it had all been a bad dream, nothing to be concerned about. But whenever he was around and she caught him looking at her in a silently contemplating way, she was reminded that it had happened—and that it could happen again.

But those moments were more than amply compensated. There were Trevor's nightly phone calls and the hours she spent visiting with her parents. They gossiped, discussed wedding plans, talked about the future and became reacquainted. Jonni found herself slipping back into her old way of life on the ranch, and discovered it fit her comfortably.

Late Wednesday afternoon, Jonni was in the kitchen with her mother. The last-minute preparations for the evening meal were under way. John Starr was there, as well, sampling the fare and generally getting underfoot.

"This tomato sauce needs something, Caroline," he decided, taking another taste from the simmering pot. "Maybe a little onion salt or some garlic."

"Maybe it needs a few less cooks." She shooed him away from the stove. "If you'd get out of our way, John, we'd get a lot more accomplished. Gabe will be coming in and we won't have the food ready to be put on the table." The front door opened and closed. "There he is now."

As heavy footsteps approached the kitchen Jonni mentally braced herself for Gabe's appearance. She barely glanced up when he entered the room, but her pulse hammered slightly louder in her ears. It was amazing how small and confined the kitchen seemed to become when he entered. Jonni felt almost claustrophobic. She shook dried parsley flakes onto the mound of mashed potatoes and concentrated on stirring them together.

"Dinner will be ready in a few minutes, Gabe," Caroline promised.

"No hurry. I still have to wash up."

"Would you like a beer, Gabe?" her father offered.

"A glass of cold water sounds better."

Gabe walked to the sink near the counter where Jonni was working and turned on the cold-water tap. The glasses were kept in the cupboard above her head. He let the water run as he opened the cupboard door and took a glass from the shelf. An electric awareness seemed to charge the air around her.

"How are you?" His drawling question sounded like a caress, as if he was making love to her with his voice.

Her gaze was forced to him. Damn, why did he

have to look at her like that? That lazy black intimacy of his eyes created havoc with her senses.

"Fine." Jonni tried to sound natural and not all tied in knots.

"If you keep stirring those potatoes, they're going to turn into a starch glue," Gabe warned in a tone heavily underlined with mockery. Then he turned to fill his glass with the running water.

Her hand stopped stirring the spoon around in the bowl. She moved away from the counter before she ruined the potatoes in her attempt to avoid Gabe.

"The potatoes are ready, mother." She made her voice sound bright. "Shall I put them on the table?"

Before she had received an answer, there was a knock at the back door. Jonni was closest and she walked over to answer it, carrying the bowl of potatoes with her. One of the ranch hands, Duffy McNair, stood on the back stoop. In his forties, he'd worked at the ranch for the past fifteen years.

"Hello, Jonni." He courteously removed his sweat-stained Stetson. "I saw Gabe coming up the walk. Can I talk to—"

He didn't have the request finished before Gabe was standing behind her. "What is it, Duffy?"

"It's Lida, that chestnut mare with the four white feet. Ted found her about an hour ago. She's in foal and been havin' a pretty hard time of it," he explained.

"In foal?" Gabe repeated. "But she isn't due for almost another full month yet."

"I know." The cowboy shifted his position,

fingering his hat. "Ted mentioned last night that she looked as if she was ready, but I knew she wasn't due yet, so I never checked on her today." His head dipped down, revealing a balding patch on top of his head. He shuffled again uncomfortably. "It's all my fault. The mare's in a bad way down there. The foal's comin' the wrong way. Ted and me have tried to turn it—he's at the barn with her now. The truth is, Gabe, we might lose 'em both."

"Have you called the vet?" Gabe didn't bother to find out where the blame might lay.

"Yeah, I called him on the tackroom phone." Duffy grimaced and lifted his shoulders in a hopeless shrug. "It's springtime, he's gotta couple of emergency calls ahead of ours. He doesn't know when he can get out here. I think you'd better come take a look at the mare."

"You say the foal is coming the wrong way?" Gabe repeated.

"That's what it looks like." Duffy shrugged again as if he was no longer certain of anything.

Jonni nearly jumped when Gabe laid a hand on her shoulder. "You've helped me a couple of times when we've had a breech birth with cows. Do you want to come?"

"Yes." Her agreement was an automatic thing. A ranch depended on its animals. When something was wrong with one of them, all individuals were obligated to help. That was a lesson she had learned while growing up.

"What about you, John?" Gabe asked. "We might need your experience."

"I may have the experience, but I don't have your instinct with animals, Gabe. I'll trust your judgement in any situation," her father conceded. "If you find you need me, I'll come."

Gabe took the bowl of potatoes from Jonni's hands and passed it to Caroline. Duffy was already starting down the steps.

"I'll keep dinner warm," Caroline Starr promised.

"You and dad go ahead and eat," Jonni said as she walked out the door ahead of Gabe.

"And don't worry about keeping the food warm for us," he added. "Jonni and I don't mind eating cold food."

As the trio walked swiftly down the worn path to the barn Gabe's hand rested on the small of her back to usher her along. Jonni realized just what she'd let herself in for—possibly long hours of close association with a man it would be wisest to stay away from. She tried to forget about the male hand resting on the sensitive area of her back and to think only about the mare waiting for them at the barn.

"Damn, I'm sorry about this, Gabe." Duffy McNair apologized again, his hat firmly on his head again, concealing the bald spot.

"That mare has a history of easy foalings. You couldn't suspect that this time there would be complications or an early birth," Gabe insisted.

"At least she's in the barn," Jonni offered in consolation. "We could be walking out to the pasture."

"I knew you'd find a bright side to this." Gabe

smiled down on her and her heart did a leaping somersault.

"Yeah, if the mare don't die," Duffy muttered under his breath, instantly sobering both of them.

Inside the barn, two drop cords ran parallel to an end stall where electric lanterns illuminated the wood-partitioned enclosure. Ted Higgins, the slim, bowlegged man Jonni had met briefly on the weekend, was inside with the mare. He was stripped to the waist, breathing heavily from exertion, perspiration gathering in the hollows of his collarbones. When he saw Jonni accompanying Gabe and Duffy, he self-consciously reached for the shirt draped over the manger and hurriedly put it on.

"How is she?" Gabe paid little heed to the man as he knelt beside the mare lying quietly in the straw. Jonni stood beside him, ignoring Ted while he buttoned his shirt.

"She ain't good," Ted admitted. "Her breathing's too shallow, no steady pulse. I've been trying to turn that damn—darn foal, but the legs keep gettin' in the way and...." His voice trailed off lamely in defeat.

The chestnut mare was lathered from her labor, her shiny coat damp with sweat. She made a whickering moan and Gabe stroked her wet neck.

"Easy, girl," he crooned softly. Jonni saw the grimness in his eyes when Gabe glanced at Duffy standing just inside the stall door. "Get me some soap and fresh water, preferably warm." The mare made another low sound, plaintive and weak, which tore at Jonni's heart. "Take it easy, girl," Gabe soothed. "We'll see what we can do about getting things straightened out. You just rest and

save your strength for later on when we'll need it."
He ran an exploring hand over the mare's extended belly then straightened.

"What do you think?" Jonni asked anxiously.

"I don't know yet." He shook his head in a
troubled way.

Duffy returned with a bucket of water. "Luke-
warm. It's the best I could do," he said.

Tossing his hat to Ted, Gabe began unbuttoning
his shirt. There was a queer tightness in her throat
as Jonni watched him shrug out of it and saw the
overhead lights play across the rippling muscles in
his back. His hard flesh was tanned a deep copper
and rough, curling dark hairs covered his arms and
part of his chest. Realizing how avidly she was
staring, Jonni turned back to the mare and knelt
beside her head to whisper calming sounds. She
listened to the sound of splashing water as Gabe
washed.

When he'd finished, he walked back to the mare
to kneel in the straw. "Okay, little lady," he said
to the mare. "I'm going to see if I can't help you a
little here."

Jonni ran her hand slowly along the mare's neck
and continued to talk to the horse in a low, soothing voice. The mare was now taking rasping short
breaths, dangerously exhausted. Jonni cast anxious glances at the competent, thorough man
working swiftly to do what he could for the mare.

"I'll be damned!" A sudden grin alleviated the
stern concentration in his expression.

"What is it?" Jonni held her breath. Had he
found what was wrong?

"No wonder you were having trouble, Ted,"

Gabe said, still wearing that smile that held more than hope. "You should have started counting legs. There are two foals here, both trying to get born at the same time. Now—" he grunted slightly as he strained "—if we can just convince them they have to come out one at a time, we'll be all right."

"Are they both alive?" A smile was starting to spread across Jonni's face, as well. The birth of twin foals was an event.

"Alive and kicking." Beads of perspiration were forming on his forehead, tufts of black hair clinging to the moisture. "Both of them."

The heavy silence that had dominated the stall suddenly lifted. Glances were exchanged all the way around, bright, hopeful looks that lightened the atmosphere. Even Duffy's face, which had been gloomy with guilt, was now wreathed with a smile.

"Get me some rope, Duffy," Gabe ordered. "If I can get hold of the two legs of one foal, we'll try to repel the one and make the way clear for the other." Duffy was gone and back in quick time. They all watched as Gabe struggled and strained to achieve his goal. Perspiration glistened over his skin, muscles flexing in undulating swells of power. Here was the combination Jonni had told Trevor about, strength, skill and intelligence— brawn and brains.

"I've got it," he murmured, and relaxed for a minute to catch his breath. His gaze pierced Jonni. "Do you understand what I'm planning to do?"

"Yes, I think so," she nodded.

"Come and give me a hand, then," Gabe ordered. She moved to kneel beside him and help. "You take the rope and turn the backward foal around while I pull the other foal out," he instructed.

In unison, they worked in conjunction with the mare's weakening contractions. The strenuous task within close quarters involved physical contact. It was unavoidable. Yet Jonni was only conscious of the strength that flowed from his hard, warm body into hers.

When the tiny hooves and wet face of the first foal made their appearance, a low cheer was raised by Duffy and Ted. Large, luminous brown eyes blinked at Jonni, whose muscles were trembling from her effort. From somewhere in the depths of her reserve she found the strength for a weak laugh of joy. A few seconds later the foal was lying in the straw and Duffy was tenderly wiping it dry.

"One down. One more to go," Gabe declared tiredly, and smiled at Jonni. "I'll take over."

She scooted out of his way, weary but revived by a happiness she'd never know before. Leaning against the side of the stall, she watched the coming of the second foal. Without the obstacle of its twin, the birth was easy.

"A pair of fillies," Duffy announced, "as pretty as their mother."

"How's the mare?" Gabe asked, slowly pushing his tall frame upright.

"You just give her a few minutes and she'll be investigatin' those little girls of hers," Ted stated with a proud-papa look.

Jonni tore her gaze away from the delicate perfection of the foals to watch as Gabe walked to the bucket of water to rinse himself off. He'd saved the mare and her foals, but she knew no one would congratulate him for it—it was part of his job. But it contained its own built-in reward system, those two tiny creatures in the stall, the beauty of birth.

There was no towel to dry on, so Gabe reached for his shirt. He saw her looking at him and smiled. Tugging his shirt on over his wet skin, he made no attempt to button it. When he walked toward her Jonni rose guiltily to her feet. She hadn't exerted nearly as much effort as he had, nor worked for the length of time that he had. She was sitting and he was standing, a circumstance Jonni immediately changed.

When Jonni stood up, the mare rolled upright to gather her legs under her. After one shaky attempt to rise, the chestnut mare succeeded in getting to her feet. Turning her head, she pricked her ears toward the foals and whickered softly.

A bit intimidated by their strange new world, the foals blinked at the sound. One curled back its lip and emitted a squeaky answer. The mare turned in the straw and lowered her head to investigate the pair.

"Sugar and spice and everything nice, that's what they're made of, Lida," Gabe told the mare. Whether he was aware of it or not, Jonni knew he had just named the foals.

"They're beautiful." Jonni made the obvious and unnecessary comment.

His arm moved behind her to cross diagonally

from shoulder to waist, his hand cupping her hip-bone. It was a silent communication of a shared experience and the wonder of it. Jonni automatically curved an arm behind his broader waist to complete the quiet linking together. It seemed a very natural thing.

"Look," Gabe instructed.

An awed and waiting silence stole through the four members of the audience. Straw rustled beneath miniature hooves as the foal with the spot of white on its forehead made its first attempt to stand on its toothpick legs. The mare nudged her encouragement after an initial collapse. The foal tried again. Its head made it top-heavy and its legs were too long, but it would grow into both in time.

With a precarious lunge the foal wobbled on all four feet. Immediately its little broom tail began swishing the air in a signal of victory. It was evidently the sign its twin had been waiting to see, because it then made its first attempt. The mare blew softly, communicating with her offspring in the low sounds coming from her throat.

A smile tugged at Jonni's mouth at the pathetically uncoordinated attempts by the twin foals to walk. Their spindly legs couldn't seem to decide which direction was their final destination. But there was a big lump in her throat, too, at the wondrous and age-old scene of mother and babies.

Instinct guided the foals to the mare's flank with a couple of helpful nudgings from her, their knowledge part of nature's marvel. They suckled hungrily, heads butting, legs wobbly, tails swishing.

"I guess this little family don't need us anymore," Duffy declared, and walked toward the door leading out of the stall into the barn's interior walkway.

"Yeah, we might as well be goin' to get our own supper," Ted agreed. "Here's your hat, Gabe." He handed him the hat. Respect and admiration gleamed in the look he gave Gabe.

Gabe took the hat and set it on the back of Jonni's head. "See you in the morning, boys."

"Good night," Jonni added, feeling intimately close to Gabe but not threatened.

"Good night."

Listening to the sounds of their footsteps fading into silence, Jonni made no move to leave the stall or the close, comfortable position beside Gabe. There was too much peace and contentment where she was for her to be anxious to leave it.

"Hungry?" His one-word question was spoken quietly.

"No." Jonni matched his tone, not wanting to break the spell. "I'd forgotten what it was like to watch something being born, to be a part of it."

"The miracle of life."

She nodded. "It's happening all the time. It's such a constant thing, yet it's always so new."

Jonni continued to watch the mare and her foals. "That's what makes having babies so wonderful."

"I suppose you plan to start a family immediately." An undercurrent of harsh violence threaded its way through his comment.

A sudden tension electrified her nerves. She felt instantly defensive against the hurt his words caused. She tried to laugh, but it was a brittle sound.

"Don't forget I have a career, Gabe," she reminded him with false brightness. "It's going to last for several more years yet. A model can't risk ruining her figure—or her future—by carrying a child."

"You'd be in your thirties."

"Yes, I know." Jonni was aware of the potential risk involved at that age, and she tried not be frightened of it, to appear happy and unconcerned.

"How large a family would you like to have?"

Out of the corner of her eye, Jonni saw the downward tilt of his chin as Gabe turned to study her. "Four, five, half a dozen," she wished aloud before cold reality made her add, "but I'll settle for one healthy baby."

"How many children does Trevor want?" There was something in his voice that indicated Gabe knew he was asking a loaded question.

Her head jerked up. "Why do you always have to read between the lines?" she choked, a mist of tears stinging her eyes. Her gaze ricocheted from his narrowed look as she blinked away the moisture and struggled to maintain her poise.

"He doesn't particularly want any children, does he?" Gabe persisted, challenging her to answer his question.

She wouldn't admit that. "He'd like to have a son," she said. "Maybe I'll just have to keep trying until I get it right." Her attempt to inject humor failed miserably.

The invisible force of Gabe's anger seemed to

fill the silence. "He'll grudgingly accept one child and you want a brood. As incompatible as the two of you are, you're going to have a hellish marriage if you go through with it." His voice rumbled on a low, ominous note.

"They say opposites attract," Jonni defended, frightened by the picture he was painting. She kept trying to imagine Trevor holding their child, but she kept having visions of the baby spitting up on his silk tie.

In a movement rife with suppressed rage, Gabe grabbed her shoulder and turned her to face him. "You little fool, opposite personalities attract only when they complement each other. When the hell are you going to open your eyes?"

But she had opened them. And she was being consumed by the dangerous black fires burning in his look. Her defenses were being melted away by their overpowering heat. She was only dimly aware of the grim line of fury thinning his mouth and tautening the muscles along his jaw. A savage despair seemed to flicker in his eyes.

"How could any man not want you to have his children?" Gabe demanded with harsh softness.

He pulled her inside the circle of his arms and crushed her to his chest. His chin rubbed against the side of her forehead as his hand, stroking the back of her hair, nestled her head in the hollow of his shoulder. His embrace offered comfort and support and Jonni was weak enough to need it, feeling pummeled and torn apart by emotions she couldn't understand.

"Break the engagement, Jonni, before it breaks you," he warned thickly.

"But I'm going to marry him," she protested in a pained whisper.

There was nothing to separate her from his bare chest. Unbuttoned, his shirt hung open. Beneath her hands his flesh was vital and firm; his chest hairs were rough against her cheek. He smelled of soap and straw and, most of all, the vigorous male odor of himself. The hard feel of Gabe was a sensation she was becoming addicted to.

A work-callused hand roughly caressed her cheek as Gabe tipped her head up. His gaze skimmed over her face in a heavily lashed look which lingered on her parted lips.

"How the hell do I get myself into these situations?" he muttered. "I've got to be the biggest damn fool ever born."

"No, I am," she corrected breathlessly.

In the next second his mouth was silencing her and dizzily sweeping her to a new emotional high. A wild kind of rapture raged in her breast. She felt it echoed by the thud of his heart beneath her hands. Her skin felt feverish wherever his caressing hands touched her. Desire became an aching torment that arched her soft curves to fit his unyielding male contours.

Forsaking her lips, his mouth moved its ravishment to her neck. His strong white teeth nibbled at its sensitive cord. Jonni shuddered against him with the sweet intensity of longing and softly moaned his name.

"Damn it, Jonni, I'm too old for this," he groaned, rubbing his cheek against hers in agitation. "Kisses aren't enough to satisfy my sexual appetite anymore." His hand covered her breast, demanding an intimacy and sending a shaft of dangerous pleasure into her being. "I want to make love to you. I want to feel your silken flesh naked against mine, Jonni. I want to satisfy your needs."

"D—Don't ask me, Gabe." The first seed of panic began to grow, a rigidity entering her boneless shape.

"What does that mean?" His hands dug into her flesh punishingly. "Am I supposed to take you without giving you a chance to say yes or no? Or is that a no?" He sounded cold with control.

Jonni had been uncertain of her meaning before, but his taunting words made it definite. "It's no." Shakily, she pulled out of his arms and turned away so her expression wouldn't reveal how easily her mind could be changed.

Gabe stood watching her for a tense moment, breathing hard. Swearing roughly, he reached down and picked up his hat, which had tumbled from her head. He dusted it against his leg to knock the straw off it, then pulled it low on his head. Out of the corner of her eye Jonni saw him start to button his shirt. His glittering eyes caught her look.

"If the sight of a man's chest disturbs you, maybe you'd better look the other way," he suggested with hard cynicism and buttoned his shirt halfway before tucking it into the waistband of his Levi's.

"You have every right to be angry," Jonni admitted. "It was my fault and I'm sorry."

"You're sorry?" Gabe repeated sardonically.

"If you think I'm going to apologize, you're crazy as hell."

There was a flash of temper in her jeweled eyes. "Damn it, Gabe, I'm trying to—" What? She stopped, not knowing what she was trying to accomplish.

Gabe measured her with a look. "Yeah, maybe it's time you explained what you're trying to do," he challenged.

"Hello?" Her mother's voice dragged out the questioning call. "Gabe? Jonni? are you still in here?"

Jonni was saved from his question. "Over by the lights, mother," she answered.

Two sets of footsteps approached the stall. Duffy just told us the mare's had twins," her father spoke up. "Caroline and I came down to see them."

Stopping outside the stall, the Starrs leaned against the sides of the manger to look at the newborn foals. Luckily, there wasn't much conversation required from either Jonni or Gabe as Caroline made exclaiming phrases over the equine family. Jonni was entrapped by an unbearable tension; a brittle shell surrounded her. And Gabe, who rarely showed expression, looked more tight-lipped than usual.

"You two are probably starved by now," her mother declared, sighing as she pushed away from the manger wall. "I have a pot of soup warming on the stove and a plate of sandwiches on the table. You'd better come to the house and eat before you faint from hunger."

Jonni's gaze slid briefly to Gabe before she walked swiftly past him to the stall door. Her stomach was a churning mass of nerves. Food was the last thing she wanted, but she didn't want to go into a lengthy explanation of that fact to her parents.

"That sounds good, mom," she lied.

"Aren't you coming, Gabe?" her father frowned as Gabe remained where he was.

"No." His answer was abrupt. "I'm tired. I've lost my appetite somewhere."

Her steps faltered, but Jonni resisted the impulse to glance at Gabe. She smiled at her parents and saw the funny look her father was giving her. "That's all the more food for me, isn't it?" she joked. She wanted to run out of the barn, but she restrained her pace to match her parents'. As she left with them, she felt Gabe's eyes burrowing into her back.

CHAPTER EIGHT

A FEW MINUTES PAST ONE on Friday afternoon, Jonni led the saddled dun gelding from the barn. The sun felt almost hot on her back and the air was deadly still. She swung into the saddle and turned the horse toward the corral gate. Gabe was on the other side of the enclosure, mounted on a big, muscled bay, its coat gleaming like polished mahogany. He had just started to ride out from the ranch yard, but at the sound of her creaking saddle leather he reined in the head-tossing bay horse to look back.

It was impossible for Jonni to alter her course. With squared shoulders, she rode to the corral gate and bent to unlatch it. Gabe watched, obviously waiting for her. Pushing the gate open, she rode the dun through the narrow gap, then reined it backward and to the side to close the gate, never hurrying in her motions.

"I just got done warning the boys, so I might as well tell you, too." Gabe spoke when she had finished. "From now on, there'll be no smoking when we're out on the range. Or if you have to have a cigarette, make damned sure it's out."

Jonni frowned and walked her horse toward his. "Why?" His warning wasn't an idle one. Something had prompted it.

"There was a grass fire near town this morning," he told her grimly. "Fortunately it was spotted right away and they were able to contain it."

"A grass fire at this time of the year?" Her expression was incredulous. "My God, what's it going to be like in the summer?"

"Hell, if we don't get some rain." He reined the nervously eager bay toward the open land.

"Where are you going?" Jonni asked.

"I'm riding over to the Cimarron to check on the cattle." Gabe seemed to hesitate before he added, "You're welcome to come with me...if you want." His voice was cruel in its indifference.

"I might ride partway with you." She tried to match his tone.

One shoulder rose to indicate he couldn't care less and he sent the bay forward at a long, tireless trot. Jonni urged her mount into the same gait, feeling angered by his attitude instead of relieved.

Gabe took the lead and Jonni followed to one side, her horse's nose even with the cantle of his saddle. He paid no attention to her. On a level stretch, his horse broke into a ground-eating canter, and Jonni's horse was quick to follow.

The faster pace generated a breeze that evaporated the perspiration on her neck and cooled her skin. Her long blond hair was tucked beneath the crown of her hat, a few wisps escaping to curl around her collar. She pulled the front brim lower on her forehead to shield her eyes from the glare of the sun.

Despite the lack of communication between them, Jonni found a certain companionship in riding over the red-tinted hills with Gabe. There was a destination ahead of her instead of an aimless wandering ride. With this inner satisfaction, she began enjoying the rugged vistas provided by the land they traveled through. If her gaze strayed more than once to the wide shoulders of the taciturn man riding with her, she told herself it was only natural.

As they neared the banks of the Cimarron River, Gabe slowed the tall bay horse to a walk. The dry, yellowing grass swished beneath their striding horses to accompany the creaking saddle leather and jangling bits. The stock cows were scattered over the land, some grazing, others chewing their cud. White-faced calves bawled for their mothers at the sight of the riders, but most lay sleeping in the sun.

They stopped at the edge of the riverbank. Below them the current was sluggish, the water rusty with the red earth of its riverbed. Jonni stared at it for several seconds.

"I don't ever remember seeing it that low before," she commented.

"I know," Gabe agreed tersely.

"What are you going to do?" She glanced at him.

He lifted his gaze, narrowing it at the southern sky. "Pray that those clouds aren't one of nature's practical jokes."

Jonni looked in surprise at the thunderheads building on the horizon. She hadn't noticed them before. "They came up fast. It might be a storm."

"Let's hope that's not an empty prophecy," he

offered dryly. "It's hot. We'd better give the horses a breather."

By the time Jonni had dismounted Gabe was on the ground, loosening his saddle cinch. She did the same and the zebra dun emitted a rolling snort of pleasure. Gabe led his horse into the scanty shade of a tall cottonwood tree, its limbs just starting to bud with leaves.

Pulling on the reins, Jonni walked her horse over and tied it to a piece of deadwood so it could graze. Gabe leaned against the tree, bending a knee to rest his heel against the trunk. He lifted a hand to his shirt pocket as if wanting a smoke, only to remember the restriction he had imposed and return his hand to his side.

"The cows look as if they're in good shape," Jonni observed. A meadowlark sang from off to her left.

Gabe didn't comment on her remark. Tipping his hat to the back of his head, he let his gaze run over her face, the slimness of her neck and the rise of her breast, leaving her with the sensation that he had touched her.

"When you were growing up, what was your idea of marriage?"

The unexpectedness of his question made her stiffen. "I don't think I want to get into that kind of discussion with you," she said tensely.

"I didn't ask what your expectations are now," Gabe pointed out. "Only what they were when you were younger."

"I suppose I thought it would be like my parents' marriage," she answered to show she wasn't afraid, "with the wife cooking the meals, cleaning the house and working in the garden."

"And children?" Gabe prompted.

"Yes, and children." Irritation flared that he should bring up that subject again.

He didn't pursue that particular topic. "Did you want to live in the city or the country?" he asked instead.

"In the country, of course," Jonni retorted, "like my parents. Where I could have horses and a place to ride. That's all I knew, so naturally it's what I expected."

"After spending the past six years in New York, you prefer a home in the city," Gabe concluded. "An apartment, I should say," he corrected.

"No, I don't prefer it." She felt the stirrings of unease. "I would like to have a house in the country, but with Trevor's business interests, it's more convenient for us to live in the city."

"Whither thou goest, I will go," he mocked. "How noble of you to sacrifice!"

"Listen, if you're going to start in on this again, I'm—" Jonni began in agitation.

"Don't listen to me," Gabe interrupted. "Listen to what you're saying. You want a home in the country where you can get up with the sun, and children that you can tuck into their beds at night. You want to be a wife and mother, not a person whose image is plastered on every magazine cover. Is that the kind of life lover boy is offering you?"

"I know what kind of life I'll have with Trevor and I've accepted it." She began twisting the huge engagement ring on her finger, conscious of its heavy weight.

"Have you, Jonni?" Gabe asked in low challenge. "Have you accepted the fact that you'll never be totally content for the rest of your life? It's a shallow existence he's offering you compared to the kind of fulfillment you want."

"I can be happy with it," she insisted.

"Can you?" Gabe was skeptical.

"What do you care?" She flung him a shimmering blue glance, her voice rising sharply as her composure snapped, but she could no longer endure his baiting of her.

A deadly stillness settled over him. There was a cold and ruthless look in the gaze he leveled at her. His silence was more unnerving than any of his previous comments. It was a relief when he finally spoke.

"You deserve a beating for that remark."

"And I bet you'd love to be the one to give it to me, too." But Jonni averted her gaze before Gabe could regard that statement as an invitation. "None of this is really any of your business," she said stiffly. "It's my life."

"And you're on the brink of making an unholy mess of it," Gabe informed her in a grim tone. "There were times when we could talk things out. You used to come to me for advice. Now you won't even listen to reason."

"It isn't the same anymore." She swung her gaze back to look at him helplessly. "Things are different between us."

The sharp breath he exhaled held cynical laughter. "At least you're intelligent enough to recognize that."

"This isn't fair." A tumultuous upheaval was going on inside her.

Jonni hugged her arms around her stomach and stared at the ground, fixing a misty gaze on the blades of grass near the dead tree limb her horse was tied to. She'd never be able to recapture that supreme confidence and joy for her engagement she'd felt when she arrived. Gabe had created doubts where there had been none.

"I almost wish I'd never come back," she said tightly.

"Believe me, Jonni, there have been times when I've wished you hadn't, too." His agreement was cool and sardonic, flicking her like a whip.

From the south came the rumble of distant thunder. Jonni lifted her gaze in its direction. The clouds had moved in to block out the sun and cast a solid shadow over the terra-cotta buttes and mesas. Lightning splintered inside the billowing, gray black clouds, electric and intense.

"Do you think we're in for a storm?" she asked Gabe, not satisfied with her opinion of the threatening look of the clouds. He had already pushed away from the tree to walk to his horse.

"There are no bees around. The flies are sitting." He draped a stirrup over the saddle seat and began tugging at the cinch strap to tighten the saddle. "I haven't seen any birds in the sky for the past five minutes. It's going to storm. If we don't want to get caught in it, we'd better head for the ranch."

Feeling his calm urgency, Jonni hurriedly tightened the cinch on her own saddle. The signs of nature he had observed made her aware that he had been cognizant of all that had happened around them while she had been so wrapped up in their conversation she hadn't noticed a thing. She glanced at the parched earth.

"I hope we don't get caught in a downpour," she said. Gabe was already in the saddle and waiting when she mounted.

"I'm not worried about getting wet," he replied ominously, and dug a heel into the bay's flank to send it bounding forward into a canter.

Another rumble of thunder was muffled by the drumming of the horses' hooves as Jonni urged her horse into a fast canter after Gabe. They traveled swiftly, trying to outrun the clouds taking over the sky. The thunder rumbled closer, lightning flashing behind them.

They were halfway to the ranch when the first fat raindrop struck Jonni. It was followed by a second and a third. Thunder clapped the clouds and the rain splashed down. Her horse tugged nervously at the bit, trying to break into a gallop. She held it back, sparing a glance from the rough terrain to look at Gabe.

The much needed rain had come. There was a rejoicing light in her eyes to match the smile on her lips, but there was no such answering expression on his profile.

Her horse made a shying lunge sideways as lightning crashed nearby. Jonni felt the reverberation of the deafening thunder in the air. The wind came to whip the rain into sheets, soaking her clothes and plastering them against her skin.

One blinding flash of lightning was followed by another and another until the air around her seemed charged with electric particles. Danger heightened her senses as Jonni realized they were likely targets for the jagged bolts of fire.

"We've going to have to take cover!" Gabe shouted above the thunder. It rumbled and vibrated the earth like a herd of stampeding cattle. "That way." He pointed to an outcropping of sandstone ahead of them.

At the base, the sandstone had been hollowed by the elements. Altering their course they raced for the crude, cavelike shelter. The overhanging ledge that formed the rock roof was tall enough to enable them to ride under it, escaping the deluge of rain and splintering lightning.

The zebra dun snorted and danced nervously as Jonni dismounted. The recess carved into the sandstone formation wasn't very deep, but it was some twenty feet in length. There was room enough for the horses to stand side by side and be protected from the rain, except for what the wind drove in. Steam rose faintly from the heated flesh of the horses, wet from the downpour.

"Whew! That was some ride!" Jonni declared with a breathless laugh, revived and invigorated by the exhilarating flirtation with danger. "My clothes are saturated." She plucked the sodden material of her blouse and held it away from her rib cage to show how wet she was.

Gabe looked. And in that brief, black glance,

Jonni was made aware of the revealing way her blouse had molded itself to her thrusting breasts. The wet material was almost transparent. A scorching heat licked through her veins.

But there was no reference to her suggestive appearance when he spoke. "You look like a young girl with your hair tucked under your hat like that." He took the dun's reins from her hand and turned away. "There's a dry rock over there. You might as well sit where you can be out of the rain."

A chunk of flat sandstone rested near the recessed wall of the cliff. Jonni walked over to it, subdued, while Gabe tied the horses to a stubby bush. Removing her hat and sitting on the rock, she shook her hair free. It tumbled about her shoulders. Because it had been protected by the hat, her hair was only partially damp, its blond color darkened by the faint moisture. At a wicked crash of lightning she looked out.

"How long do you think the storm will last?" she asked as Gabe walked over to where she was seated.

"It's too violent to keep this up for long." Although there was room on the rock, he made no attempt to sit with her. Instead he towered beside her, intimidating her with his size. He reached into his shirt pocket and took out the makings of a cigarette. He glanced down to see her watching him. "Do you remember how to roll a cigarette?" There was something gentle in his glittering look, a remembrance of old times, more companionable occasions.

"Yes, I think so." She nodded, warmed by the memories of when Gabe had taught her how.

"Show me." He passed her the tobacco and a dry cigarette paper.

Smiling confidently, Jonni took the makings from him. Gabe crouched beside her, sitting on his heels and balancing effortlessly on the balls of his feet. She formed the rectangular piece of paper into a trough and tapped a mound of tobacco into the center. With her fingertip she spread the shredded brown leaves along the paper trough.

"Am I doing it right?" She glanced brightly at Gabe as she lifted it to her mouth to lick the edge of the paper.

Before she could succeed, Gabe was reaching to take it from her. "You'd better let me do it." Part of the tobacco spilled as he took the paper from her hand.

Stunned by his abrupt behavior, Jonni frowned at him. "Why? What was I doing wrong?" She was certain she had been doing it correctly.

"Nothing." He licked the paper and rolled it around the tobacco. "I'd just forgotten what the sight of that pink tongue of yours could do to me."

Striking a match, he cupped the flame to the end of the cigarette between his lips. Jonni sat motionless, shaken by the injection of disturbing intimacy into the conversation. A turbulent, elemental tension raced through her. It had no connection to the savage storm raging around them. In agitation she rose to face the rain whipping into their crude shelter. She felt excited, confused and unnerved all at the same time.

"Why did you have to say that?" she demanded of Gabe in a thin, taut voice.

"It's the truth." Gabe straightened to stand at her shoulder. "Why shouldn't I have said it?"

"Because." She flung the weak, unsupportable reason at him.

The freshly lit cigarette was arched into the storm. "Why does it bother you to know I'm aroused by you?" Gabe wanted to know. When Jonni tried to avoid his intent regard, a finger turned her back to face him and remained beneath her chin. "It isn't just the pink tip of your tongue. I'm aroused by the way the firm roundness of your breast fills my hand, the way your hips fit perfectly against mine, and the sexy, animal sounds you make in your throat when I arouse you."

"I don't!" Jonni denied the last.

"You do," Gabe insisted and drew her into his arms to prove it.

Thunder rocked the ground beneath her feet but Jonni didn't know the difference between it and the tremors of desire that shuddered through her system. The lightning paled in comparison to the golden flame his devastating kiss ignited.

Her fingers sought the silken smoothness of his slick wet hair. His hat got in the way of her curling fingers. In absent awareness, Gabe reached up and deftly flicked it to the back of the wall. Then his hand was back on her spine, arching her into the ever tightening circle of his arms.

The wind whipped in stinging droplets of water to pelt her cheeks, but Jonni was oblivious to the storm. She was out of control, existing only because Gabe was holding her, kissing her, touching her, caressing her. Yet not even that was enough.

She wanted more. A hungry, whimpering sound came from her throat.

Gabe pulled his mouth from her lips to drag it near her ear. "Did you hear that?" he taunted. "That wild little mating sound you made."

Turning and twisting, Jonni's lips sought to regain possession of his mouth, but he eluded her. "Yes," she moaned at last.

"Do you make sounds like that for him?" he growled against her throat.

"Gabe, please!" She didn't want to make comparisons, not at a time like this. Trevor had been an expert in the art of love, but he'd never turned her bones into putty the way Gabe was doing.

In a burst of feline aggression she forced her hands inside the collar of his shirt and dug her nails into the hard flesh of his shoulders in an effort to assert her own needs and end the torment of his elusive mouth. She heard the sharp intake of his breath and felt the flinching of his muscles.

"Tell me, damn it!" He nipped the sensitive skin at the base of her neck in retaliation.

"It was never like this, Gabe," Jonni admitted in a breathless whisper. "Never."

He shuddered violently against her, as if some last barrier had finally been breached. Her admission was rewarded with a bruising kiss that made the previous moments seem less of a torment. Jonni responded to its blazing ardor with complete abandon. Gabe's hand forced aside the material of her blouse to seek the roundness of her throbbing breast.

Then he was dragging her to the ground as if

caught in an undertow that not even he, with all his strength, could withstand. Jonni knew the glorious feeling—she was the subject of emotions too powerful to deny or resist.

The searing longings had her writhing and twisting beneath him as his mouth sought the dusty rose tip of her rain-moistened breast. Her fingers tugged his shirt open so she could feel the bareness of his fiery skin against her own. His mouth murmured her name over and over again as it moved against her throat, her ear, her cheek and finally her lips. His weight crushed her slim body onto the hard ground.

Lightning split open the sky in front of the cavernlike shelter. The dun horse neighed in alarm and strained against the tied reins. Its rear hooves danced backward, black-striped legs bumping into the entwining pair on the ground. Reacting with catlike reflexes, Gabe rolled Jonni out of reach of the trampling hooves and continued the same fluid movement onto his feet.

"Easy, boy, easy." His husky voice attempted to quiet the horse. "Easy, now."

The gelding was on the verge of bolting. Jonni sat up, shifting out of its possible path and drawing the front of her blouse closed. Gabe laid a hand on the tan rump and walked slowly to the horse's head. It rolled its eyes and snorted, but didn't elude the hand that reached for the reins. The ends were still tied to the branch, broken from the bush.

While Gabe remained there to quiet the horse, Jonni shakily began to button her blouse and tuck it securely inside her jeans.

Staring at that virile figure of manhood, she knew she wished the interruption had happened much later, after the ache in the pit of her stomach had been satisfied. And she was shattered by how willing she was to cast aside the laws of morality and fidelity she had been raised to respect. It simply wasn't possible to be in love with two men. Yet there she was, engaged to one man and eager to make love to another.

She rose to stand on weak legs, and the movement attracted Gabe's attention. Absently patting the horse's neck, he retied the reins and walked back to her. His hands moved to hold and caress the soft flesh of her arms. The smoldering light in his eyes told her he wanted to take up where they left off, and the temptation was sweet agony. Her hands rested naturally on his waist, but she didn't sway into his arms.

"I'm engaged." Troubled confusion and want shimmered in her eyes.

His dark gaze discarded its lazy, seductive look to widen in mockery. "Are you reminding me of that? Or yourself?"

Jonni winced as that gibe struck a vulnerable nerve. Her gaze dropped to the tantalizing hollow at the base of his throat. She absently studied the sinewy cords in his neck.

"There are so many things..." she began, and wearily shook her head. "I'm finding it all difficult to understand."

His grip tightened to demand her undivided attention. "I love you, Jonni." A muscle twitched in his jaw. "What's so difficult to understand about that?"

"No." She shook her head, not wanting to believe him, wary because she knew how much more complicated it would all become if he was telling the truth.

"Yes." The laughing sound he made lacked humor. "I love you. I've been in love with you for years. Half the time I've been like a rutting stag without a doe. And the other half. . . the rest of the time, it's been pure hell."

The shock of his confession whitened her face. "I don't believe you. Not all this time."

"From almost the moment I set eyes on you," Gabe told her, his jaw hardening. "You were fourteen and your boyish figure was just beginning to fill out. But you were beautiful even then. I tried to convince myself it was your beauty that fascinated me, but within a matter of months I knew it went a hell of a lot deeper than that."

"No." Jonni pulled out of his hold, rejecting everything he said. "It isn't true. You never so much as hinted to me, not even that time when I—"

"When you developed a crush on me," Gabe interrupted to complete her sentence. "You'd barely turned fifteen then, Jonni, and I was twenty-eight. Believe me, I was tempted to nurture that juvenile adoration, but I couldn't trust myself to be satisfied with the innocent affection you wanted to give. So I trampled it into the ground and prayed that I could arouse it again when you matured into a woman."

In a gesture of agitation Jonni combed her fingers through the side of her hair. Gabe had always been skilled at hiding his thoughts, she knew this, but she was frightened by what he was revealing.

"In the meantime," Gabe continued, his narrowed eyes watching her changing expression, "I had to listen to all your boy talk about your dates, how many times your boyfriends kissed you and whether they were any good at it or not. Your adolescent love life nearly drove me insane with jealousy."

"Why?" She turned on him, half-convinced but still doubting. "Why didn't you ever indicate that you were interested in me? Not in the beginning, but later on, when I was older."

"I did. When you were seventeen, I decided I'd waited long enough. I went to your father and told him—"

"You went to my father!" The ground seemed to rock beneath her feet. "He knew all this?"

"Yes," Gabe admitted evenly. "I told him I was in love with you and that I wanted to start asking you out, if he had no objections."

Had her father kept Gabe from coming forward, she wondered. "Did he?"

"John had his doubts. I was a good deal older than you, and considerably more experienced. But he respected me for coming to him first before making my interest known to you. He gave me his permission."

Jonni was thoroughly confused. "Then why didn't you ever ask me out?"

"I did."

"When?" she challenged.

"You'd just had an argument with that Jefferson boy who played football," Gabe began.

The memory came flooding back. "And you said you'd take me to the dance that Friday if I wanted to go," Jonni remembered, her eyes widening in astonishment.

"As I recall, you turned me down flat, insisting that you weren't *that* desperate." His eyes were cold as they remembered the exact words of her rejection.

"I . . . I thought you were joking," she defended, "that you were just offering to take me because you felt sorry for me. I never dreamed . . . ."

"No, you never did," he agreed flatly. "So I decided to wait a little longer until you finally looked at me and saw a man instead of a convenient shoulder to pour your troubles on. Unfortunately you got that crazy notion in your head to become a model and you took off for New York."

"I never could understand why you were so violently opposed to my going," she said in a marveling voice of discovery. After all this time, it finally made sense. "You kept insisting I'd hate New York and I'd never succeed."

"And the more I kept telling you that, the more determined you became to prove I was wrong. Every time we got into an argument over your leaving, I knew I was driving you into going, but I was too damned much in love with you to keep my mouth shut." There was a haunting agony to his tightly clipped admission.

"I never guessed, Gabe," Jonni murmured.

"No, I know you didn't. Which meant I still

had a chance. I kept waiting for you to come home. A half a hundred times over the past six years, I've made up my mind that I was going to fly there and bring you back, but I never did. I told myself that if you were the woman for me, you'd come back. I even made a try at forgetting you." His mouth quirked in cynicism. "But I couldn't walk by a newsstand or pick up a magazine without your face staring back at me."

"I did come back, though." She had the feeling she was seeing Gabe for the first time, a man with deep, abiding emotions, strong and unshakable, a rock in a windswept desert.

"Yes, you came back. When I saw you step out of that plane, I didn't know if I was dreaming or whether it was really you. I'd been waiting for so long I thought my mind had snapped."

"But when I kissed you hello, you nearly broke my ribs pushing me away," Jonni accused, finding his actions that day at odds with his confession.

"Pushing you away?" He laughed at that. "It was all I could do to keep from crushing you in my arms and never letting you go!" His expression sobered to a grim look. "Then you introduced lover boy as your fiancé. I've never come any closer to killing a man in my life." He grasped her shoulders in a punishing grip. "You aren't going to marry him, Jonni."

Under the spell of his disturbing touch, Jonni believed he was probably right. But so many of the things she had believed had turned out to be so wrong. Maybe this crazy, wild fire Gabe had kindled would burn itself out and there would only be cold ashes left. This past week had made chaos of her life.

"I'm too confused to be certain about anything." All her insecurities played across her expression, tousled gold hair sweeping her shoulders with the bewildered shake of her head.

"I love you. You can be sure about that." He lowered his dark head and took her mouth, kissing it deeply. Jonni was again swept breathlessly into the emotional current of his passion, which carried a pledge of eternity. When the pressure of his lips became seductive, she struggled against his persuasive force. Gabe let her escape his kiss, but not his arms. "All I want you to do is love me just a little."

"I need time to think," she protested, and fought the impulse to admit she already cared for him too deeply for her peace of mind.

His jaw was clenched as he suppressed the surge of impatience that flashed in his eyes. It was as if he knew how easily he could physically arouse an answer that would be more satisfactory to him.

"How long?" he demanded.

"Not . . . long," Jonni promised. She wanted to make her decision when she was free from the unsettling influence of his touch. And she needed to reevaluate her feelings for Trevor.

"It had better not be." Gabe released her and took a step away. He seemed to need the distance between them as much as she did. "I don't know how much more of this I can stand." He pivoted toward the horses. "The lightning has moved on. I think we can risk riding back to the ranch."

"All right." Jonni silently agreed that there was greater danger in remaining where they were.

Bending, Gabe picked up her hat as well as his own and handed it to her. She took it and swept her hair on top of her head, pulling the hat over it. While she tucked a few wayward strands under the crown, Gabe untied the horses and turned them outward. He held the dun's bridle while she mounted and then passed her the reins. Jonni waited under the protective overhang as he swung into his saddle.

The rain was still coming down steadily but the wind had died and the lightning flashes were a considerable distance away. The thunder was a gentle roar. The horses moved reluctantly at their riders' bidding into the rain, their hooves clip-clopping on the wet ground.

CHAPTER NINE

THE BARN DOOR STOOD OPEN. Ducking her head, Jonni rode the gelding inside out of the rain. Gabe had paused to close the corral gate and was only a few feet behind her. Water dripped from the crease of her hat brim as she dismounted, her toes squishing in wet socks, her leather boots saturated inside and out.

"I'll take care of the horses." Leading his horse, Gabe reached for her reins. "You'd better go and change into some dry clothes." His gaze didn't quite meet hers.

"Gabe?" There was something she wanted to ask him. Or tell him. Jonni wasn't sure which. She just knew she didn't want to leave him yet.

He turned back to her, and something written in her expression snapped the thin thread of his control. With a stifled groan he caught her in his arms. It must have been what she wanted because she immediately wound her hands behind his neck and met the downward descent of his mouth halfway.

The heat of his body warmed her rain-chilled flesh, which shivered beneath her wet clothes. His deep, langorous kiss swelled her heart to the bursting point. The thought of never feeling this mindless joy again made her cling to him with desperate fingers. If this was love, she didn't want to lose it.

"So this is what's been going on while I've been gone!" A voice as sharp and cutting as a broadax sliced them apart.

Jonni looked in disbelief at the man standing just inside the doorway, his legs spread slightly apart, his hands clenched into fists at his sides. Her pulse drummed an alarm, its message beating wildly in her throat.

"Trevor!" The shock of identification was in her voice. Her gaze ran to Gabe, who had pivoted at Trevor's cold challenge. He stood a half a step in front of her, partially shielding her. The wet shirt, plastered to his skin, revealed tautly coiled muscles ready to spring.

"If you remember my name, maybe you also remember that I'm your fiancé," Trevor said in cold, sarcastic condemnation.

"What are you doing here?" Jonni breathed the question, her feet rooted to the barn floor. Part of her kiss-dazed senses was beginning to assimilate the potential danger in the situation.

"Surely it's obvious. I came here to be with you for the weekend." Trevor's eyes never stayed on her long. They kept flickering to Gabe, aware of where the opposition stood and of the threat he represented.

"Why didn't you let me know you were coming?" she demanded in agitation. If she'd had any advance warning at all of Trevor's arrival, the atmosphere wouldn't be crackling with such violent undercurrents.

"I wanted to surprise you. Some surprise!" he

jeered. "I flew in ahead of the storm, only to discover you'd gone riding. Or at least that was what your father said. He failed to mention that you'd gone riding with *him*."

"He didn't know," Jonni protested, not wanting Trevor to think her father had any knowledge of the change in her relationship to Gabe.

"I went out to check the cattle," Gabe said in an emotionless voice that made Jonni's blood run cold. "At the last minute Jonni decided to ride along with me."

"And to think that while I've been pacing the floor, half out of my mind with worry over you out there in that storm, you were with *him*!" Trevor had begun to tremble visibly with jealous anger.

"We would have been back sooner, but when the storm came up we had to take shelter," Jonni explained. Considering Trevor's present state, she had the feeling she was wasting her breath, but she had to make some attempt to keep this scene from erupting into something ugly.

"That must have been cozy," he taunted.

"Nothing happened." Jonni knew how close that statement had come to being a lie, and her complexion crimsoned at Trevor's skeptical glance. Almost immediately it swept to include Gabe.

"I had a feeling all along about you, Stockman," Trevor accused in a curling sneer.

"Isn't that a coincidence?" There was something reckless and dangerous in Gabe's coolly amused response, all pretense of politeness discarded. "I'll bet I had the exact same feeling about you."

Her heart catapulted into her throat. She was being left out of the conversation, ignored. The two men were now regarding each other with open challenge, their eyes locked in combat, each trying to stare the other down.

"I've always suspected the code of the West was just a myth—the honest, hardworking cowboy with all his supposed righteous morality for another man's property." Trevor was blatantly contemptuous. "You're nothing but a thief, trying to take something that doesn't belong to you."

"I'm not the thief." Cold steel ran through Gabe's voice. "Jonni was wearing my brand long before she ever met you."

A cold chill of inevitability shivered through her veins. It was snowballing out of control. Jonni was powerless to slow the momentum that was racing to a final confrontation. There seemed nothing she could say to prevent it.

Trevor laughed, a cold, deadly sound that came from his throat. "I'll bet you'd like to believe that. You probably had it all worked out, didn't you, Stockman? If you could marry the rancher's daughter, you could get your hands on the whole operation. You wouldn't be just the hired hand anymore."

Jonni stopped breathing. That remark was a direct insult, a slap at Gabe's pride. A deadly stillness enveloped Gabe. She was reminded of a cougar, poised to leap on its prey. Any hope that there was something she could say or do to stop this vanished.

When Gabe finally spoke, it was with a calmness that said he found a certain satisfaction in the situation. "I sincerely hope you're prepared to back that up, Martin, because I'll enjoy making you retract that statement."

Trevor hesitated for only an instant. "You're damned right I'm prepared to back it up." He started forward, shrugging out of his suit jacket as he walked toward Gabe.

"No! Stop this!" Jonni grabbed at Gabe's elbow in a desperate appeal.

His eyes never left Trevor as he removed her hand from his arm and pushed her to one side. "Stay out of the way, Jonni," he told her. "This is going to be a pleasure."

Blindly, Jonni retreated until she came up against the rough lumber of the barn wall. Her hands were pressed against the surface, indifferent to the splintering texture scraping at her palms as she watched the scene unfolding before her eyes.

With rare disregard for the care of his clothes, Trevor tossed his suit jacket toward the corner of the barn and began tugging the knot of his silk tie loose. Never once did he slow the deliberate strides that carried him toward Gabe.

"The first time I met you I thought you were an insolent devil." With the tie thrown aside, Trevor unfastened his collar button, and two more. "I wished then that I'd rammed my fist down your throat. I should have. This time I will, you can count on it."

Gabe never said a word. He just waited, flat-footed, for Trevor to walk up to him. At the last minute he ducked under Trevor's swing, the blow glancing off his shoulder, and hooked a fist into

Trevor's midsection. Trevor grunted and blocked the following right to his jaw.

Paralyzed by the action, Jonni couldn't look away. Trevor was no match for Gabe—she knew it. Gabe had the weight advantage, was stronger and had a longer reach. It was all stupid and senseless, but she seemed to be the only one who realized that.

Jonni winced when Trevor staggered under Gabe's fist and came back for more. An overhand punch snapped Gabe's head back and Jonni saw blood trickling from the corner of his mouth. Trevor had drawn first blood, but that didn't mean he'd win the fight.

After an exchange of more smashing blows, Trevor was knocked to the ground. Jonni watched him rise. There was a gash across his cheekbone and a thin trail of red from his nose. She wanted to scream at him to quit, to give up before he was badly hurt, but she knew Trevor wouldn't hear her—and if he did, he wouldn't listen.

Halfway to his feet, he lunged at Gabe. Gabe sidestepped the first blow, which carried the full force of Trevor's weight behind it, and rocked under the second before landing a punch of his own. Both men had begun to breathe heavily, grunting with each swing. The brawling sounds had the stabled horses whickering nervously and shifting in their stalls, adding to the noise.

A right from Gabe sent Trevor sprawling on the floor near the opposite wall. As Trevor staggered to his feet he grabbed a pitchfork propped against the wall. Jonni's gaze widened in horror.

"Gabe! Look out!" She shouted the warning.

Even as she called out, Trevor was swinging the pitchfork like a baseball bat, apparently unaware of the lethal, pointed prongs weighting the end. Gabe's raised forearm warded off the blow then twisted to grab hold of the weapon. While Trevor fought to keep possession of the pitchfork, he left himself open for Gabe's right cross. It knocked him backward onto the floor, tearing the wooden handle from his grip.

Gabe turned and speared the pitchfork into a small mound of hay in the corner. Cold anger darkened his expression as his attention returned to the half-conscious man in the blood-splattered and dirty silk shirt. Trevor was trying to rise. Gabe reached down to grab him by the front of his shirt and haul him to his feet, and the savage intent written on his face ended Jonni's silent role as spectator.

"No. No!" In a frightened rage, she flung herself at the arm Gabe had cocked to swing. "You're going to kill him! Stop it!" She beat at him, aware that her ineffectual blows were inflicting little damage. "Stop it, you big brute!" she screamed at him. "Can't you see he's hurt? Leave him alone!"

"I'm finished with him." Breathing heavily from the brawl, Gabe let him go.

Trevor swayed drunkenly and would have fallen if Jonni hadn't rushed to his side to support him, taking his weight. Trevor made a weak attempt to push her aside without success. Her hand lightly and soothingly stroked his jaw as she turned his head to look at her. His eyes were glazed over, betraying his barely conscious condition.

"It's over, Trevor," she whispered to him, an ache in her voice. His handsome, chiseled face was bloodied and bruised and no trace of his cocky self-confidence remained. "You're hurt. You can't fight anymore." He stopped resisting and leaned heavily on her. He was beaten and knew it. Her flashing eyes turned on Gabe in accusation. "Just what did you prove?" she challenged, almost choking on the sob that rose in her throat.

There was a dangerous narrowing of Gabe's black eyes. The back of his hand was pressed to his mouth, half covering his mustache. When his hand came away there was a smear of blood on his skin, but Gabe hadn't taken the abuse Trevor had received.

"He sweats and bleeds just like the rest of us," Gabe answered, and reached to pick up his hat from the barn floor.

"You're nothing but a brute and a bully!" Her voice quivered. "You knew you could beat him. You knew you were stronger and faster, but you just had to let him provoke you into fighting. Trevor wasn't any match for you, and you knew it. You challenged him!"

"He didn't have to take me up on it."

"You know he did!" Jonni accused.

"Instead of rehashing how the milk got spilled, you'd better do something about taking care of lover boy," Gabe suggested dryly. He hesitated a fraction of a second, his hands on his hips, then he added, "I'll help you get him up to the house."

"No!" Jonni rejected his offer of assistance with an angry toss of her head. "I don't need your help, and Trevor wouldn't thank you for it. You've done enough damage without humiliating him still more by dragging him to the house for mom and dad to see."

"Jonni, I—" Whatever Gabe had been on the verge of saying, he clamped his mouth shut on it, a jaw-tensing hardness in his expression.

When he failed to make a retort to which she could answer back, tears welled in her eyes. A puzzled anger and hurt made her throat ache, and she lashed out at him in frustration. "I don't understand you...I don't understand either of you! It was senseless and stupid to fight. What kind of satisfaction could you get out of hitting each other?"

"It was strictly a personal satisfaction," Gabe answered grimly. "You see, Jonni, we didn't have anything to lose. One of us had already lost you before the fight ever started." Flat, expressionless black eyes made a slow sweep of her. "I don't see why you're so upset. Women get a kick out of men fighting over them."

"It's revolting to see anyone getting beaten up," Jonni denied in a flash of anger.

Trevor lurched against her and her arms tightened to steady him. "My legs don't want to stand up," he murmured in a dazed voice.

Her heart contracted at the sight of the bruised and swelling face reeling close to hers. "Ssh, darling!" She soothed him with her voice, treating him like an injured and confused child. "I'll help you."

With a gesture of weariness Gabe pulled his hat low on his forehead and turned away. "Take him up to the house before he bleeds all over you."

Jonni glared at the callously indifferent man walking to collect the saddled horses. His total lack of sympathy for his defeated opponent angered her, but Gabe wasn't paying any heed to her.

"Come on, Trevor." She shifted her attention to the wobbling man leaning against her. Draping his arm over her shoulder, she turned him toward the barn door. "Let's go to the house and treat those cuts and bruises on your face."

Trevor tried to make his legs obey, but his was a staggering walk that relied heavily on Jonni for both support and direction. The ground, muddy from the heavy rain and continued drizzle, didn't provide solid footing for either of them. Jonni slipped and slid, half carrying Trevor. The sprinkling rain ran down her hair and into her eyes, hampering her vision and making the short journey even more difficult. By the time she reached the front porch of the house she was panting from the exertion.

"We're almost there," she promised Trevor, and gathered herself for the effort of pushing the door open and maintaining her balance at the same time.

Turning the knob, she kicked the door open with the toe of her boot. She was trying to maneuver Trevor across the threshhold when her father appeared in the foyer. Bewildered astonishment opened his mouth and drew a frown on his forehead.

Jonni didn't have time for explanations at the moment. "Help me get him inside, dad." The strain of her burden echoed itself in the gasping request for assistance.

But John was already hurrying forward to steer Trevor into the house and add the support of his arms. One look at the battered face and he shouted, "Caroline!" Then his gaze slashed questioningly to Jonni. "What happened? He looks as if he ran into a brick wall."

"It was Gabe," she said stiffly.

An eyebrow arched. "That's the same thing," her father muttered, almost to himself. "Let's take him into the kitchen," he directed.

"Good heavens, John, what's the panic?" her mother inquired in a laughing voice as she rounded the doorway of the dining room, wiping her hands on her apron. She didn't require an answer when she saw Trevor. Having been a nurse before she was married, she was instantly all crisp efficiency and bustling concern. "I'll get some warm water and the first-aid kit. Bring him to the kitchen."

Together Jonni and her father took him to the kitchen. A basin of warm water was already on the table, along with clean towels and an antiseptic. The first-aid kit was opened and Caroline Starr was removing the items she felt she might need.

When they had him seated in a chair, Caroline handed Jonni a small bottle with its cap removed. "Here, give him a good whiff of this ammonia. That should bring him around."

Jonni held the bottle to his nose. When Trevor gasped and started coughing, she took it away. "Enough," he insisted in a more lucid voice.

Shouldering Jonni aside, her mother took over to bathe the blood from his face and check the seriousness of his cuts. She asked Trevor a list of clinical questions about his vision, his hearing, any dizziness or nausea. Jonni stood beside his chair and watched, exhausted and shivering in her rain-soaked clothes. Her father pressed a cup of steaming coffee into her numb hands.

"He's all right," he said. "You go change out of those wet clothes before you come down with pneumonia. Your mother will see to him."

After a second's hesitation, Jonni tiredly submitted to the commanding tone of his voice. She walked out of the room to the stairway to the second floor and her bedroom, nursing the strong, sweet coffee. As she started up the stairs, her father caught up with her.

"What does Gabe look like?" he asked, partly from concern and partly from curiosity.

"What do you think?" Bitterness crept into her voice. "He's hardly got a mark on him." The fight's outcome had been predictable and it still irritated Jonni that Gabe had found it necessary to prove it.

In her bedroom Jonni finished her coffee while the bathtub was filling with hot water. After the bath she towelled her hair damp-dry and changed into a kelly green sweater with ivory slacks. Half an hour from the time she had left the kitchen, she was walking back downstairs.

Trevor was in the living room. A thin strip of bandage covered the cut above his eye. A larger one was on his cheek, but it didn't totally conceal the purpling bruise surrounding the gash. An ice bag was alternately being applied to his cheek and to his split and swollen lip. Jonni paused at the doorway, then walked in.

"How do you feel?" she asked with quiet concern, aware of how he looked.

"The way any man feels when he's on the losing end of a fight," Trevor answered testily. "Like an ass."

"You shouldn't. It was wrong of Gabe to fight you when he knew he could win," Jonni insisted with a harsh undertone.

"Look at this." He tipped his head back and carefully parted his lips. "He knocked a chip off my front tooth." There was a black gap in the row of even white teeth.

"I'm sorry, Trevor." Jonni wasn't sure why she was apologizing.

"I'm glad I have a good dentist." He grimaced and pressed the ice bag to his lip. "I'm just sorry I ever picked a fight with him."

"So am I." She stood close to his chair, too ill at ease and upset to sit down.

He caught at her left hand, looking up at her with a warm light in his brown eyes. A smile was too painful for his injured mouth. "At least I have the consolation that his victory was a hollow one. You're here with me."

Jonni wasn't certain it meant anything so she kept silent. His fingers twisted the diamond ring she wore, unnecessarily reminding her that she was engaged to him. He pulled her down to sit on the arm of his chair.

"I suspected all along that Stockman wasn't to

be trusted. I had a feeling he'd try to make mischief, but it didn't do him any good." Trevor was placing all the blame on Gabe and treating Jonni as an innocent participant, which she knew she hadn't been.

"Trevor—" Her attempt to correct that misconception was interrupted.

"You don't have to worry about him anymore," he assured her. "I've made arrangements for the chartered plane to pick us up at nine in the morning, and I have our airline reservations confirmed to New York. I've talked to your parents. They quite understand that it's best, under the circumstances, for you to cut your vacation short."

He was taking it for granted that she wanted to go with him. Since Jonni wasn't sure whether she wanted to or not, she said nothing. There would be time enough to make up her mind between now and tomorrow morning. Trevor seemed unperturbed by her silence as he affectionately squeezed her hand.

"Would you mind going into the kitchen, darling, and seeing if your mother can fix me something to drink, preferably with a straw?" he asked.

"Of course not," she answered, and straightened from the chair, slipping her hand from his light hold.

As she walked to the kitchen, Jonni was aware that his touch had done nothing for her. His caress had not sparked a savagely sweet rush of emotions. There had been no odd tremor of excitement.

Her mother was at the kitchen sink peeling

potatoes when Jonni walked in. Caroline glanced up, her look faintly anxious. "Trevor told us you were leaving in the morning."

"Yes, I know." For the time being, Jonni didn't contradict the statement. "He'd like something to drink. Would you take it into the living room for him?" She continued through the kitchen and paused at the back door where a yellow rain slicker was hanging from a hook.

"Where are you going, Jonni?" A knife and a half-peeled potato were set on the porcelain drain board of the sink.

"I want to see Gabe."

"Is that wise, dear?" Caroline frowned.

"I hope so." Jonni sighed and fastened the last of the snaps before stepping outside into the drizzling rain.

Pulling the vinyl hood over her head, she started off across the path straight for Gabe's living quarters in the renovated bunkhouse. She stopped at the door, fighting the twisting uncertainties in her stomach, and knocked twice, loudly.

"Come in." His voice was muffled by the thickness of the door.

The interior of the quarters was austere. A small kitchenette was on one side, birch cabinets built around the stove, sink and refrigerator. A small wooden table with two chairs stood next to another wall. With the exception of a floor lamp beside a leather recliner, the rest of the space was taken up by a desk and several filing cabinets. A short hallway ended in a closed door. Another door in the hallway stood open. Light streamed out and Jonni heard the sound of running water. She walked toward it, pushing the rain hood back.

Naked from the waist up, Gabe was standing in front of the sink in the bathroom. He didn't turn around when she appeared in the doorway, but glanced into the mirror above the sink where her reflection joined his. Without speaking, he finished rinsing the washcloth, then dabbed it at the cut at the corner of his mouth, wincing slightly. His knuckles were swollen and faintly discolored. On the back of his left hand there was a gash that looked sore and angry.

There was a closed expression to his face. "Did he live?" he asked dryly.

His baiting tone made Jonni snap, "No thanks to you!" The sight of him bare to the waist was making her all nervy. "You broke off part of his front tooth," she accused.

"Really?" Gabe flexed his injured hand as if realizing the source of the wound.

This wasn't the conversation she wanted to have with him at all. She took a calming breath and tried to start again. "Trevor is sorry he fought with you."

"He probably is," he agreed smoothly, and reached for a towel to dry his hands.

There was too much complacency in his response and her temper flared. "You could apologize, too." The blame was just as much his.

Gabe turned around to face her, completely controlled and impassive. "I've never walked up to anybody with my hat in my hand, and I'm not going to start now." A clean shirt was hanging on the doorknob. Picking it up, he slipped a bronze arm in one long sleeve and shrugged into the other. His gaze lightly skimmed her taut features.

She tried to goad some reaction out of him, unable to tell what he was thinking or feeling and needing to know. "Trevor is leaving for New York in the morning. He expects me to go with him."

Gabe buttoned his shirt. "Naturally he wants you to go with him. Since you're still wearing his ring, he obviously still considers you his fiancé."

Frustration welled at his noncomittal response. "Don't you care whether I'm leaving with him or not?" Jonni demanded with a faintly desperate ring.

"You know where I stand. The next decision is yours. Either you stay or you go." Gabe tucked his shirt in his pants as if they were discussing some trivial subject instead of their future.

His indifference hurt. She wanted to be told more than just that she knew where he stood. She wanted Gabe to say he loved her and wanted her to stay. She wanted to be persuaded. She wanted him to sweep away any supposed resistance with a crushing embrace.

"What if I told you I was going?" Jonni challenged.

"Are you?" There wasn't even a flicker of emotion in his steady gaze.

"Yes!" she declared out of sheer perversity.

"Then there isn't anything more to be said, is there?" A pair of impersonal hands moved her out of the doorway so he could walk past.

Shocked by his calm acceptance of her supposed

decision, Jonni could only watch as Gabe walked to his desk. He sat down in a creaking swivel chair and opened a ledger book. From a sheaf of notes he began writing down figures in the columns.

Feeling lost and forlorn, Jonni pulled the yellow hood over her head and walked numbly to the door. Her hand closed over the cold metal of the doorknob.

"Goodbye, Jonni," Gabe said with an air of finality.

"Goodbye," she choked.

With a muffled cry like a wounded animal, she jerked open the door and fled into the gray drizzle.

THE NEXT MORNING Jonni stood at the bedroom window overlooking the front of the house. Her clothes were all packed in the suitcases standing at the door waiting to be carried downstairs. It was half-past eight and the chartered plane was due at nine. She'd heard Trevor go down fifteen minutes ago but still she waited, nibbling at her forefinger.

At the sound of a motor, her hand came away from her mouth and Jonni brightened anxiously. The pickup truck rolled up to the sidewalk leading to the front door of the house. The driver got out and her heart fell to her toes. It was Duffy McNair who would drive them to the airfield, not Gabe. Her last hope faded.

On wooden legs she walked to the hall door, picked up the two lightest suitcases and proceeded down the stairs. Duffy was standing with her father in the entryway. Their voices hushed when she approached.

"Let me take those for you, Jonni." Duffy stepped forward to relieve her of the suitcases.

"I'll carry these," she insisted. "There are two more, heavier ones, upstairs in my room. I'll let you bring those." She tried to sound light and uncaring, but her voice came out artifical and brittlely gay.

"Be glad to." He began mounting the stairs on bowed legs.

"They're sitting right by the door," she called after him, then turned to her father. "Where's Trevor?"

"He took his bags out to the truck. Let me carry one of those for you," he offered.

"No. You aren't supposed to be carrying heavy things," Jonni refused.

."Don't be pampering me," John Starr reproved. "My heart isn't in such bad shape that I can't carry a few tubes of lipstick." With that, he took the cosmetic case from her hand and opened the door. Trevor was standing by the truck, along with her mother. Jonni paused at the porch steps while her father closed the front door.

"Where's Gabe?" she asked, trying not to sound too interested as her gaze scanned the ranch buildings. "I thought he'd be here this morning to see us off."

"He went to a livestock auction today." John's sidelong look was narrowed and sharply questioning. "I thought you'd said your goodbyes yesterday. Didn't you?"

"We did." Her voice wavered. With gritting determination, Jonni steadied it. "Yes, we did."

A quarter of an hour early, the plane was circling the field to land as Duffy came out of the house with the rest of Jonni's luggage. In a numbed state, Jonni submitted to her mother's hugs, kisses and tears and her father's fierce hug and gruff wish for a safe trip.

Their farewells to Trevor were more restrained and less emotional. He looked worse that morning. His bruises had colored into vivid purples and yellows. One quarter of his lip was half again as large as the rest of his mouth. The chipped front tooth added to his battered appearance.

Duffy was careful to avoid looking at Trevor when he slid behind the wheel. Jonni suspected Duffy found the sight of that bruised face amusing, but she was too wrapped up in her own misery to care about any slight, implied or otherwise, to Trevor.

The ride to the airfield had always seemed such a long one, but this time it was incredibly short. Much too soon, her luggage was being stowed in the baggage compartment of the twin-engine aircraft, its motors idling in readiness for flight. Before she climbed aboard Jonni took one last look, hoping against hope that Gabe would suddenly arrive. When she hesitated, Trevor hurried her inside.

Automatically she buckled her seat belt while staring out the window at the hangar. The plane began taxiing and she continued to watch, a strangling tightness encircling her throat. At the end of the runway the plane made its roll down the grass strip and lifted off. A few minutes later she saw her parents standing in front of the house and waving at the plane banking northeast.

Trevor leaned over. "I know you'll miss them, but they'll be coming to New York in less than a month's time to help you get ready for the wedding." His hand covered the balled fist in her lap. "We'll be married soon, darling. The next time we come back here for a visit, you'll be my wife. And you won't have to worry about that Gabe Stockman ever bothering you again."

"Shut up, Trevor." Jonni turned her head and stared out the window, letting the first teardrop fall.

CHAPTER TEN

THE STEREO MUSIC WAS LOUD. It had to be in order to be heard above the noise of an apartment full of people, all laughing and talking at the same time. A portable bar, borrowed from a neighbor, was the center of attention, drawing nearly as big a crowd as the buffet table loaded with snacks and goodies. Streamers draped the ceiling, their festive colors dulled by a haze of cigarette smoke. A huge sign hung across one wall; emblazoned on it were the words We'll Miss You, Vickie.

"Excuse me." Jonni inched her way through the crowd around the buffet and added two more platters of finger sandwiches to the assortment of hors d'oeuvres.

"Hey!" As she turned away, someone grabbed her left hand. "What happened to that sparkler you've been wearing and dazzling all our eyes with?" Her laughing inquisitor was Dale Barlow, a photographer Jonni had worked with on several occasions.

"I returned it." She shrugged diffidently and tried to withdraw her hand from the clasp of his fingers. She didn't want to remember how difficult it had been to convince Trevor she didn't want to marry him.

"Hey, gang!" Dale refused to relinquish his hold of her hand and held it aloft. "We may be losing Vickie to the lure of smoggy California, but her roommate, the beautiful Jonni Starr, is footloose and fancy-free again. She's ditched her tycoon lover boy."

Jonni winced at the phrase, the color washing from her face. She wasn't footloose and fancy-free, not by any means. She was too poignantly aware of the mistake she'd made by leaving the ranch instead of staying with Gabe, but her stubbornness had gotten in the way. She wanted to go back, but she needed more courage—more courage and less pride.

"Enough, Dale." She removed her hand from his amidst the cheers that followed his announcement. "You're interfering with the hostess while she's on duty."

"Very well. More champagne and caviar, my good woman," he requested in a falsely deep voice before breaking into laughter.

Presented with the opportunity, Jonni slipped away into the relative quiet of the compact kitchen. She was relieved to be in charge of the farewell party for her roommate. It meant she was occupied with an endless array of things to keep the party running smoothly and didn't have to pretend to be enjoying the festive air.

The doorbell rang as she was opening the refrigerator door. Jonni had discovered early on in the evening that her ears seemed to be the only ones attuned to the sound. She removed the tray of biscuit wafers topped with caviar and set it on the counter. Smoothing a hand over the front of her long black pinafore gown, she walked back into the crowded living room.

"Jonni! I haven't had a chance to talk to you all evening!" Within seconds of entering the room, Jonni was cornered by a former model friend turned actress. "Don't you have a drink?" The girl turned to the man beside her. "Bob, get Jonni a drink."

"Don't bother, Bob," Jonni refused, and backed toward the door.

"Where are you going?" The girl frowned. "We haven't had a good gossip in ages."

"Later, maybe," Jonni stalled, and motioned toward the apartment door. "The doorbell is ringing. Late arrival, I guess."

"It's ringing? How can you tell with all this racket?" The girl laughed.

An answer wasn't required as Jonni smiled and continued on her way to the door. Its buzzing ring came again, insistent in its tone. Jonni schooled her expression into a welcoming smile and opened the door.

Her heart somersaulted into her throat, lodging there to deprive her of speech. Gabe stood outside—at least it looked like Gabe, unless she was hallucinating. His broad-shouldered frame was clothed in a tailored suit and vest of dark blue with a striped tie of blue, gray and gold to blend with the pearl-gray shirt he wore.

The clothes didn't belong to the levi-clad Western man she knew, but the sun-hardened features looked the same. The neatly trimmed brush of black mustache was there, and the black hair was in its natural casually rakish style, which some men paid the earth to achieve. The bold blackness of his eyes could belong to no one else. Yet Jonni was afraid her own eyes were deceiving her. It had only been two weeks since she'd seen him. How could he have changed so much?

"Gabe?" she questioned hesitantly, half-afraid she would blink and he'd disappear.

"Hello, Jonni." The vibrant, caressing pitch of his voice flowed warmly over her. His gaze strayed behind her to the noisy party. "You've having a party."

"Yes." She was dazed, joyously mesmerized by the sight of him standing there at her door. "It's a farewell party for my roommate. She's moving to California."

"May I come in?" he asked with faint mockery.

A wave of self-consciousness rouged her cheeks. She wanted to fling herself into his arms and shut out the party but the moment had passed when she could do that. She opened the door wider and stepped aside.

"Of course, please come in, Gabe. You'll have to forgive my manners," she apologized with a nervous laugh. "When I answered the door I didn't expect to see you there."

"I wanted to surprise you," Gabe admitted, hardly taking his eyes off her.

"You succeeded. It was the best surprise I've ever had." She found herself drowning in the black pool of his gaze. She kept remembering how he had said that he once intended to come to New York to bring her home. That had to be why he was here now. It had to be! And her heart soared at the heady implications of that. The shimmer of untold happiness was in her returning look.

Gabe moved closer until there was barely the width of a hand between them. His hands rested in light possession on the curve of her slender waist. The stood in the midst of the party, but Jonni was deaf and blind to everything but him.

"Your father mentioned that you'd broken your engagement to Trevor," he said.

"Yes." Jonni nodded once. "I did."

"Why?"

"I didn't love him." How could she, when she had fallen with love with Gabe? She would have told Gabe that, but a guest intruded into their intimate conversation...a female guest.

"Leave it to you, Jonni, to snare the handsomest hunk of man at the party," the woman chided. She turned to Gabe, her red mouth curving into an alluring smile. "I'm Cynthia Sloane."

"It's a pleasure, Miss Sloane." Gabe nodded politely to the woman and slid an arm around Jonni's waist to curve her to his side.

"Aren't you going to introduce him to me, Jonni?" the woman prompted.

"This is Gabe Stockman. He's—" Jonni was unsure how to identify him "—the general manager of my father's ranch and other holdings." Jonni settled on a generalized introduction.

"Gabe." The brunet repeated the name, rolling it over as if tasting it. "Is that short for Gabriel—as in Gabriel, come blow my horn?" she asked with deliberate suggestiveness.

"No, it's Gabe, short for Gable as in Clark,"

Gabe stated in a tone that wasn't amused. "You'll have to excuse us, Miss Sloane. I have some family business to discuss with Jonni."

"Lucky Jonni," the woman replied with a pout of envy before she moved away.

Jonni did feel lucky—extraordinarily so. And proud, too. Cynthia had made her aware of the admiring looks Gabe was receiving from the other, less bold female guests at the party. She'd never seen him in a group before. All the other men paled in comparison, lacking that inborn air of command.

"Is there someplace we can talk where we won't be interrupted?" Gabe asked, bending his head to speak low in her ear. "I'd suggest the dance floor, but—" an eyebrow quirked in mockery of his own suggestion "—what I had in mind was slow dancing where you just sway to the music. It won't work with that choice of songs."

"Hardly," Jonni agreed. The pounding of drums vibrated through the room like the magnified sound of a heartbeat. Her own pulse was matching the song's tempo. "We could try the kitchen," she suggested.

"Lead the way." Gabe's hand remained on the curve of her waist as Jonni moved ahead of him through the crowd. Once they were inside the kitchen the closed door muffled most of the loud party sounds. "Aren't you worried that one of the neighbors will complain about the noise?"

"It's all taken care of." Jonni smiled mischievously. "I invited all the neighbors to the party. If they're making the noise, they can't very well complain about it."

"Very clever." He chuckled.

"Yes." Her smile faded into wonderment as she surveyed Gabe anew. He looked so self-assured and relaxed in the clothes that seemed so out of character. "I've never seen you dressed like that before. You look different. Natural, but...." Jonni couldn't explain it.

"When in Rome." Gabe shrugged away the rest of the cliché.

It was Jonni who was unsure. She glanced around the kitchen, feeling the smallness of the room—and the privacy. "Would you like something to drink?" She assumed her role as hostess since she wasn't sure what other one to play. "The refrigerator is stocked with just about everything."

"I'm thirsty." He drew her toward him, his gaze shifting to her moist lips. "Like a man in the desert sun."

With a moan of surrender Jonni met his descending mouth. Her arms wound around his neck while his encircling arms crushed her against his length. The buttons of his vest made tiny imprints on her skin, but the pain and pleasure were inseparable. Gabe's thirst was unslakable. Jonni didn't care how much he drank from the fountain of her love. It was bottomless.

"Jonni!" The kitchen door opened and a blonde came bouncing in. "Oops! Sorry," she apologized as the pair broke apart.

Flushed and glowing, Jonni ran a self-conscious hand along her neck. "Was there something you wanted, Babs?"

"Mac is almost out of ice at the bar. He sent me

out here to get some. You just tell me where to find it and you two can go back to doing your thing," the girl assured them with a knowing look.

The embrace had been too torrid for Jonni to resume it in front of someone else, even if that someone else did look the other way. Besides, she felt an odd shyness about behaving so boldly with Gabe. Being with him robbed her of her poise. She slipped the rest of the way out of his arms. Her gaze skittered away from the brief contact with glittering amusement of his dark eyes.

"The bags of ice are in the coolers." Jonni walked to the insulated ice chests sitting on the floor near the table. "I'll help you. How many do you need?"

"I'd better take three." Long, blond hair swung forward as the girl bent over while Jonni started dragging the bags of cubed ice from the cooler. Babs nearly dropped the third one Jonni handed her, but rescued it at the last instant.

"Can you make it?" Jonni frowned.

"Sure," the girl insisted, and winked, "Have fun, you two!"

It wasn't that easy to walk back to Gabe after the woman had left. He was standing by the counter where she'd left the plate of wafers topped with caviar. He had sampled one and was staring at the bite-size piece still left in his hand.

"What is this?" He flashed her a wary look.

"Caviar."

"That's what caviar tastes like." A raised eyebrow indicated that he had expected something better. "You might have warned me that fish eggs are salty."

"The next time I will," she promised, relaxing slightly at the banter. "Caviar is an acquired taste, I think, like snails. Vickie, my roommate, loves caviar. I prefer peanut butter on my crackers."

"I'll remember that," said Gabe in a voice that made her heart completely skip a beat. But he didn't pursue that happy vein of implication. Instead he walked toward the refrigerator. "I think I'll take you up on that offer of a drink."

"Help yourself," Jonni said, even though he was already doing so.

Holding the refrigerator door open, he held up a bottle of Perrier. "What's this?"

"Water," she told him.

"Imported from France?" He frowned the question in skeptical amusement.

"It's very popular," Jonni grinned. "It's usually served with a twist."

"And that's all?" he mocked, and twisted off the cap.

"That's all."

"It's water all right," Gabe said after taking a swallow. "Perrier and caviar."

"That's real uptown," she laughed, then found herself wondering. "When did you get here? Why didn't you let me know you were coming?"

"I wanted to surprise you." Gabe answered the last question first. "My plane arrived three days ago."

An astonished and confused breath was expelled. "I hope you don't expect me to believe that you've been lost for three days, because you never get lost. Where have you been? Why haven't you come to see me before now?" To think he had been in New

York three whole days, and she hadn't known. It was something Jonni didn't understand.

"No, I haven't been lost." He studied the bottle for a moment before lifting his black gaze to her. "I've been touring New York, visiting all the places you mentioned in your letters home—Wall Street, the Statue of Liberty, Times Square, Central Park. I've been to a couple of Broadway shows, a concert at Carnegie Hall, the museums, eaten at the best restaurants."

"And?" Jonni prompted when he paused.

"And I've come to the conclusion that it's a great place to visit." Gabe set the bottle on the counter. There was something final about the gesture.

"But you wouldn't want to live here," Jonni finished the common ending to his statement. "No, I don't think you would, either."

"I need space around me," said Gabe, and she could almost see his broad shoulders trying to make room in the small kitchen. "I need room to breathe. I want dirt beneath my boots, red Kansas dirt, not concrete. I don't belong here, Jonni. It's as simple as that."

"I know what you mean." There was an air of serenity about her expression. It was the same discovery she had made since returning to New York. This wasn't the place she wanted to live for the rest of her life, and not just because Gabe wasn't here. She started to tell him that. "I—"

"Hey, Jonni, there you are!" The kitchen door burst open and a couple hurried in. The man was short and fairly stout. The girl with him was beanpole-tall and coltishly attractive. She was the one doing the talking, "We've been looking all over for you. Come on!"

The urgency in her demand moved Jonni toward them. "What's wrong? Has something happened?"

"Nothing's wrong," the girl sighed with exasperation. "Vickie is getting ready to open her presents and she won't do it until you're there. So come on."

Jonni glanced helplessly at Gabe. "I'm the one who's giving the party for her. I should be there," she offered in defense of the request. "Are you coming in, too?"

"No, you go ahead," he suggested with a nod, indicating that it was all right with him. "It's where you belong."

Unwilling but feeling obligated by the friendship with her roommate, Jonni allowed herself to be marched into the living room by the oddly matched pair. She was immediately pushed into the center of the party to join in the fun of watching her roommate open presents that were sometimes outrageous, sometimes practical and often imaginative.

Nearly an hour had passed before Jonni could steal away and return to the kitchen. She stopped abruptly inside the empty room. With the possibility that Gabe might have joined the party after all, she went back inside the living room and searched through the crowd of people.

There wasn't any sign of Gabe. A wave of desolation washed over her. She pressed a hand to her mouth to hold back the sob of panic and scanned the party-happy throng. There wasn't anyone that she could even mistake for Gabe.

"Hey, Jonni, what's wrong?" Babs, the girl who had come into the kitchen for the ice, was frowning at her with concern. "Don't you feel well?"

"It's Gabe, the man who was in the kitchen with me," Jonni explained, fighting to keep her voice calm. "Have you seen him?"

"No."

"I can't believe he'd leave without telling me," Jonni protested.

"When did you see him last?" Babs asked.

"In the kitchen. I came out here when Vickie opened her presents. I went back there after she was done and he wasn't there." Jonni's voice broke slightly on the last.

"Did he say he'd wait for you? Or tell you anything?" the other woman quizzed.

"No, he just said for me to go ahead and join the party," Jonni recalled. "He said it was where I belonged."

"Meaning what?" Babs smiled wryly. "That you didn't belong with him? That's a strange thing to say."

"He didn't mean that." Jonni started to shake her head to say that the idea was foolish, then a frightening thought struck her. "Did he? Just a few minutes before that we were talking about New York and he said he didn't belong here. Babs, he *has* left," Jonni said. "He's left to go home, home to Kansas."

"Jonni, I'm sorry," the girl sympathized, and laid a consoling arm on Jonni's shoulders. But Jonni had already come to a decision and was moving away. "Hey, where are you going?"

"Give my apologies to everyone at the party. I'm going to be busy packing," Jonni told her. "I'm going home, too."

BY THE TIME she had packed what she would need Jonni had missed the last plane for Kansas City that night. The next day's planes were all booked. Two days had gone by before she finally obtained a flight and made the connection to the charter company. Below her now were the red hills of the Starr Ranch.

Jonni leaned forward to tap the pilot on the shoulder. "Buzz the house."

He banked the plane toward the ranch buildings. "This run is becoming a regular thing for us," he shouted back to her. "Maybe the company should start a commuter airline service!"

"This is my last trip here," she told him. "I'm coming to a full stop this time."

The plane flew low over the buildings. The horses in the corral shied and bolted in circles around the enclosure. As the plane climbed up to landing pattern altitude Jonni saw a familiar figure step out of the barn. A smile began lighting her face.

When the plane turned on its final approach, the pickup truck was racing and bouncing over the rutted track to the airfield. Jonni's heart was thumping so loudly she could hear it above the drone of the motors. The wheels touched down and she was home.

She was sitting on the edge of her seat as the plane taxied to the metal hangar. Gabe was standing beside the pickup, waiting. There were tears of unabashed happiness in Jonni's eyes. She could barely see to climb out of the aircraft. The pilot helped her to the ground.

Gabe continued to stand there. He didn't come forward to meet her. Jonni took the first hesitant step toward him, then another and another. Then she heard his voice, his rich, vibrant voice say, "It's about time you came home."

Jonni broke into a run, flinging herself into his arms to be lifted high in the air while Gabe kissed her and whirled her around in boundless joy.

A sparrow twittered from its perch on the gutter of the metal shed. Its mate flew in to land beside it, a twig in its beak. In the drain trough was a partially built nest. The first phase of nature's cycle was beginning.

Back by Popular Demand

Janet Dailey
Americana

A romantic tour of America through fifty favorite Harlequin Presents, each set in a different state researched by Janet and her husband, Bill. A journey of a lifetime in one cherished collection.

In October, don't miss the exciting states featured in:

Title #17 KENTUCKY
Bluegrass King

#18 LOUISIANA
The Bride of the Delta Queen

Available wherever Harlequin books are sold.

Back by Popular Demand

Janet Dailey
Americana

A romantic tour of America through fifty favorite Harlequin Presents, each set in a different state researched by Janet and her husband, Bill. A journey of a lifetime in one cherished collection.

In November, don't miss the exciting states featured in:

Title #19 MAINE
Summer Mahogany

#20 MARYLAND
Best of Grass

Available wherever Harlequin books are sold.

JD-NOV

Back by Popular Demand

A romantic tour of America through fifty favorite
Harlequin Presents, each set in a different state
researched by Janet and her husband, Bill. A journey
of a lifetime in one cherished collection.

In December, don't miss the exciting states featured
in:

Title #21 MASSACHUSETTS
That Boston Man

#22 MICHIGAN
Enemy in Camp

Available wherever
Harlequin books are sold.

JD-DEC

HARLEQUIN

Romance®

**This October,
travel to England with
Harlequin Romance
FIRST CLASS title #3155
TRAPPED
by Margaret Mayo**

''I'm my own boss now and I intend to stay that way.''

Candra Drake loved her life of freedom on her narrow-boat home and was determined to pursue her career as a company secretary free from the influence of any domineering man. Then enigmatic, arrogant Simeon Sterne breezed into her life, forcing her to move and threatening a complete takeover of her territory and her heart....